The Case
of the
Teenage Terminator

Other Middle Grade Books by

 **ANGELA ELWELL HUNT**

THE NICKI HOLLAND MYSTERY SERIES

The Case of the Mystery Mark
The Case of the Phantom Friend
The Case of the Teenage Terminator
The Case of the Terrified Track Star
The Case of the Counterfeit Cash

The Case of the Haunting
of Lowell Lanes
The Case of the Birthday Bracelet
The Secret of Cravenhill Castle
The Riddle of Baby Rosalind

THE CASSIE PERKINS SERIES

No More Broken Promises
A Forever Friend
A Basket of Roses
A Dream to Cherish
The Much-Adored Sandy Shore

Love Burning Bright
Star Light, Star Bright
The Chance of a Lifetime
The Glory of Love

THE YOUNG BELIEVERS SERIES,
with Steve Arterburn

Josiah
Liane
Taz

Shane
Paige
Noah

THE COLONIAL CAPTIVES SERIES

Kimberly and the Captives

The Deadly Chase

ii

NICKI HOLLAND MYSTERIES

The Case
of the
Teenage Terminator

Angela Elwell Hunt

A Division of Thomas Nelson Publishers
Since 1798

www.thomasnelson.com

Published in Nashville, Tennessee, by Tommy Nelson®, a Division of Thomas Nelson, Inc. Visit us on the Web at www.tommynelson.com.

Scripture quotations are from the *International Children's Bible®, New Century Version®*, copyright © 1986, 1988, 1999 by Tommy Nelson®, a Division of Thomas Nelson, Inc.

Tommy Nelson® books may be purchased in bulk for educational, business, fund-raising, or sales promotional use. For information, please e-mail SpecialMarkets@ThomasNelson.com.

This is a work of fiction. Names, characters, places, and incidents either are the product of the author's imagination or are used fictitiously.

Interior: Jennifer Ross / MJ Ross Design

ISBN 1-4003-0765-1

Printed in the United States of America
05 06 07 08 09 WRZ 9 8 7 6 5 4 3 2 1

One

Nicki Holland thought nothing else in the world was quite like the feeling of giving—and receiving—Christmas presents from friends. She and her four best friends were about to exchange gifts on the floor of Christine Kelshaw's crowded bedroom, but the cramped quarters didn't diminish the joy of Christmas one bit.

Nicki sighed and crossed her long legs. "I'm so glad school's out for Christmas break. Just think—no more homework until next year!"

"I'll miss school, even though we're only out for two weeks," Meredith Dixon said. "Seventh grade has been a lot more fun than sixth grade was. Since we started solving mysteries together, I'm never bored."

"Aren't superintelligent people like you always bored?" Laura Cushman asked, settling onto the floor. "Where I come from in Georgia, we like to take things slow and easy. Life's not boring, just relaxing."

Christine grinned, her green eyes sparkling. "I know one thing that's never boring—opening presents! Kim, why don't you get us started?"

Kim Park shyly offered a small package to Meredith. "This is my first Christmas since coming from Korea," she said, ducking her head. "And the first time I have ever had such a smart friend. I am glad I drew your name, Meredith."

Meredith took the gift and methodically unwrapped it. "This is great, Kim," she said, holding up a book. "I've always wanted to read *More Ways to Increase Your Word Power*. Thanks so much!"

After flipping through the book, Meredith pulled a small package from her purse. "I drew your name, Nicki," she said, presenting the gift with a dramatic flourish. "And I know you like music, so I hope you like this."

Under the red foil paper Nicki found a jeweler's box. Inside was a dainty charm on a silver chain. "It's an eighth note," Nicki said, holding it up so it sparkled in the light. "I love it! Thanks, Meredith."

Nicki fastened the chain around her neck, then she stood up so she could peek in Christine's mirror.

"Looks great," Chris said, pulling on Nicki's shirt, "so sit down and let's keep going."

"Okay, okay." Nicki sat back down and pulled out the present she'd brought. "I drew your name, Chris." She smiled at her red-haired friend. "I wanted to get you something to remind you of the last mystery we solved."

As Christine dug into the package, paper and ribbons flew.

"Be careful, it's breakable!" Nicki said, laughing. "You'll destroy it before you even get the box open."

"It's Buttons!" Christine squealed, pulling out a ceramic figure of a Pekignese puppy that looked just like the dog they'd befriended while investigating the case of the phantom friend. "It looks just like him!"

"Since you and Buttons were so close, I thought you'd like to have something to remind you of him," Nicki explained. "Plus, I know you like dogs."

Christine impulsively threw her arms around her friend. "Thanks, Nicki. You're the greatest."

"Are you guys finished in there yet?" a voice called from the other side of Christine's closed bedroom door. "Someone else lives in that room, too, you know."

Christine made a face. "Can't you wait just a few more minutes, Torrie? There's no other quiet place in the house."

"Five more minutes," Torrie called. "Then I need to get in there. I've got to get ready for a party tonight."

Christine shrugged and looked at the others. "She'll take three hours to get ready," she whispered. "Because she's fifteen, Torrie thinks she gets to rule the room. But I guess we'd better hurry up."

She reached into her closet and pulled out a bulky package with the wrapping paper gathered and tied at the top with a sprawling bow. "I drew your name, Laura, and I didn't know what to get a southern belle who has everything. So I made you something. Torrie, Gaylyn, and I are making these to earn some money. Hope you like it."

Laura undid the bow at the top of the package and the paper fell away. Inside was a little peach basket, carefully painted with blue flowers and decorated with a stiff fabric bow.

"It's beautiful," Laura said, smiling. "These colors will be perfect in my room."

"You mean rooms, don't you?" Christine teased, remembering Laura's bedroom suite. Nicki and the others had been astounded the first time they visited Laura's bedroom, sitting room, room-sized closet, and glitzy bathroom. "Now it's your turn. Whose name did you draw?"

"I drew Kim's name." Laura retrieved a large rectangular box from behind her and pushed it in Kim's direction. "My mom and I went shopping. Hope you like it, Kim."

Kim opened the box so slowly Nicki had to resist yelling, "Just rip the paper off!" She couldn't help being curious. The box came from Burdines, which meant the gift was probably something to wear and something expensive, too. But Laura's mother could afford almost anything.

Kim parted the tissue paper inside the box and lifted out the cutest sweater Nicki had ever seen. Little people were sewn onto the front, and each of the people wore a different expression. The sweater's black background matched Kim's dark hair and would make her creamy skin glow.

Wow. The sweater was certainly different from the plain things Kim usually wore. Since her arrival at Pine Grove Middle School a few months ago, she had worn mostly white blouses and dark skirts.

"Oh," Kim whispered, hugging the sweater to her chest, "it is the most beautiful creation. Thank you, Laura, and thank your kind mother for me." Kim bowed in the Korean custom, but she did it so enthusiastically Nicki thought of the cork that had bobbed from her pole the last time her father took her fishing.

"Well, that's it," Nicki said, gathering an armful of wrapping paper from the floor. "I'm really glad, Laura, that you're going out of town tomorrow so we had an excuse to exchange presents early."

"I'm not exactly thrilled to be going to Switzerland," Laura said, still admiring the bow on her basket. "I'm sure it's beautiful and everything, but I'll miss being with y'all."

Torrie knocked on the door again, but this time she opened it, too. "Christine, I absolutely need the room now," she said. Her red hair was a shade deeper than Chris's and her freckles weren't as pronounced. Had she discovered a beauty secret to tone them down?

"We're finished," Christine answered, standing. She stuffed the last of the wrapping paper into a huge wastebasket. "You can come in."

Torrie came in and nodded at the other girls, then gave her sister a thin smile. "Kiddo, I want some privacy. Can't you guys go into the family room?"

Christine sighed. "Aren't Stephen and Casey in there? We can't talk with Tinkertoys and Lincoln Logs flying through the air."

Meredith rubbed her forehead. "Casey beaned me the last time we tried that. I got a Lego block right between the eyes."

"Then try the patio," Torrie suggested. "Gaylyn's out there drawing, but she's quiet."

"A fourth grader just wouldn't understand what we talk about," Christine said, raising her chin. "We can't hang out around her."

Torrie lifted her hands in exasperation and grabbed a hairbrush. "Well, there's nowhere else to go except the kitchen, and Tommy's in there on another eating rampage. Go wherever you want, but just go!"

Christine looked at her friends. "We could go sit on the front lawn. I think the wind is kind of cool today, but the sun's nice."

Laura cast a pleading look in Christine's direction. "I'd really like a drink of water. Can we stop by the kitchen to get a drink first?"

Christine nodded absently and led the way out of the room, as Meredith caught Nicki's eye and lifted an eyebrow. *What did that look mean?*

Two

Nicki soon realized what Meredith's glance meant. In the kitchen, Christine went to the cupboard for glasses and Nicki, Kim, and Meredith simply stood nearby. But Laura sank onto a barstool and watched Tommy, Christine's older brother, prepare a triple-decker club sandwich.

Tommy was the oldest kid in the Kelshaw clan, but only by ten minutes—he and Torrie were twins. He was the leader, though, and it was obvious by the way he carried his shoulders that he was conscious of his role. Or, Nicki thought, at least he was conscious of Laura watching his every move.

"What'cha doin?" Tommy asked Christine as she reached across him.

"I'm getting us a drink," she said. "Is that okay with you?"

Tommy looked at the girls and grinned. "Hey, don't take it out on me. I didn't kick you out of the room."

Like Torrie, Tommy's hair was more auburn than red, but he didn't have the same pale skin and freckles the girls shared. He was bronzed from the hot Florida sun and his eyes were deep brown. He was short for a guy, but well built. To the girls in the kitchen, he was a walking dream and forever out of their reach. Because he was in the tenth grade at Pine Grove High, they could only admire him from a distance.

Why didn't Christine realize how lucky she was to have Tommy Kelshaw for a brother?

Tommy noticed the girls' packages. "Oh yeah, the big gift exchange was today, right?" He winked at Laura. "Did you make out okay?"

Laura blushed about ten different shades of red, but it was Meredith who answered. "We all did great," she said, looking up from her book. "I got this great book on how to improve your vocabulary. I'm going to learn a new word every day, so that's 365 new words next year, plus if I study the root words there's no limit to how many words I can learn. It says here all I have to do is use each word in a sentence three times a day. Isn't that great?"

Tommy stabbed a four-inch toothpick through the center of his sandwich, the finishing touch. "Great," he said, grabbing his plate and heading for the family room. "Let me know when that comes out in a comic book, will ya?"

After he left the room, Laura looked up at Christine and sighed. "He's perfectly gorgeous," she said. "I couldn't even sleep if I lived in the same house with him. How do you do it?"

"Tommy?" Christine crinkled her freckled nose and let a cabinet door slam. "He's just a brother. He's okay, I guess, and I have to admit he's not as much of a pain as he used to be. Lately he's been trying really hard to impress Mom and Dad with how responsible he can be so they'll let him play football next fall."

Meredith pulled a stool over to the kitchen bar. "I thought he played football this year."

"He did," Christine answered, pouring tall glasses of ice water. "But he only played on the junior varsity team and he said it was the pits. No one came to see the games and they never got to play at night. He said even the JV cheerleaders weren't really into the games, and Tommy wants to be the best."

"I think he *is* the best," Laura said dreamily, resting her head on her hands. "You're so lucky to have a brother."

Christine snorted as she handed out glasses of water. "If you had a brother, you'd change your tune. He's turned our garage into a weight room and every time I need the bathroom he's in there taking a shower. He works out all the time. The other day Dad told him to trim the grass along the backyard fence, and he did it with the grass clippers in one hand and a five-pound dumbbell in the other." She nodded at her friends. "He's obsessed."

"A lot of guys work out," Nicki said. "It's supposed to be healthy."

Laura sighed again. "He looks wonderful."

"He could be overcompensating," Meredith said.

"Over what?" Christine asked. "Speak English, girl."

Meredith set her glass on the counter. "He may be overcompensating because he's not exactly tall. Because he's not as big as some of those guys on the football team, he may feel he has to work twice as hard to be accepted. It's a fairly common psychological response."

Nicki laughed. "Have you been reading *Psychology Today* again?"

Meredith lifted her chin. "All I did was point out an obvious truth."

Christine grinned. "Yeah, you may be right. The high school coach told him that if he worked out all spring and summer and built himself up, he'd stand a good chance against all the big guys on the varsity football team. Coach Doster signed Tommy up for wrestling and even suggested he get a personal trainer."

Laura blinked. "A what?"

"A trainer. Tommy can't afford to hire one of those professionals down at the gym, but Pops Gray volunteered to help coach him. Pops is supposed to know a lot about weightlifting, nutrition, and all that stuff."

"He sounds like somebody's grandfather," Nicki said, laughing. "Is he?"

Christine shook her head. "No way. He's a senior at Pine Grove High. Pops is just a nickname. His real name is Blane."

Kim scratched her head. "Then why do they call him Pops?"

Christine shrugged. "Where do those guys get any of their nicknames? When my dad played basketball in college, they called him Money because he had a sure shot. You know—he was always on the money."

Kim giggled. "American nicknames are strange."

"It's true," Christine said, laughing. "We still get people who call here and ask to speak to Money—the person, not the green stuff."

Laura sighed again. "Is Pops as wonderful as your brother?"

Christine lifted one shoulder in a half shrug. "He comes over all the time, but mostly he and Tommy hang out in the garage and lift weights. Mom and Dad seem to like Pops, though. He says, 'Yes, sir' and 'No, ma'am,' and you know how that impresses my parents."

Nicki looked at Laura—her eyes were half closed, so Nicki knew she was lost in a dream world. Laura was an incurable romantic.

"Pops couldn't be nearly as wonderful as Tommy," Laura murmured.

"Hey." Nicki snapped her fingers in front of Laura's eyes. "Cut it out. Tommy Kelshaw is too old for you. Besides, he has a girlfriend."

Wide awake now, Laura turned to Christine. "He doesn't, does he?"

Christine nodded. "Sorry, Chris. He's been going with Amy Trimble ever since school started. They're really tight. She's gorgeous, she's a cheerleader for the varsity squad, and she's nice, too. She's another reason why Tommy's dying to play for the varsity team."

"I am crushed!" Laura moaned, her head falling with a thunk onto the counter. "My life is ruined. Do you know how it feels to have a dream extinguished before it's fulfilled? To have a bud nipped before it has blossomed? To have—"

"—a voice stifled before a mouth is taped shut?" Meredith finished. "Come back down to earth, Laura."

Someone knocked on the kitchen door that led into the garage. "Come in," Christine called. When no one answered, Christine looked at Nicki. "Would you mind opening the door? It's probably one of the neighborhood kids coming to play."

From her stool, Nicki leaned over and pushed the back door open. Then she gasped.

A young man stood in the doorway, about eighteen, she guessed, with broad shoulders, golden blond hair, and arms that looked like they had been sculpted from granite. He was wearing shorts and a sleeveless tank top even though it was one of Florida's rare cool days.

"Hi," he said, smiling at Nicki with sparkling blue eyes. "I do have the right house, don't I? I'm looking for Tommy."

Nicki gulped. "Yes, this is the right house."

Laura, Kim, and Meredith stared dreamily at the visitor while Christine shook her head and yelled, "Tommy! Pops is here!"

"Don't bother to get him," Pops said, stepping into the house. "I'll find him."

As he walked toward the family room, the girls followed his movements until he disappeared through the doorway.

"Christine," Laura said, turning, "I don't know how you do it. I could never get used to having gorgeous guys just come walking through the house . . ."

Christine leaned over the counter to look her friend in the eye. "Laura, you've been much too sheltered."

Three

Christmas came and went, and with it the only truly cold spell Nicki could remember. For four days straight the temperature never climbed above freezing, and Nicki's mother moaned that her tropical plants would not survive.

By the end of January, though, the sun had resumed its normal intensity in the turquoise skies of coastal Florida. Nicki and her friends were glad to see the sunshine when the dismissal bell rang on Friday afternoon.

Well, everyone was grateful for the warm weather except for Kim.

"When it is so warm, it is too hot to wear my new sweater," Kim grumbled when the girls met at their lockers.

"Cold weather without snow is a ripoff," Christine said as she lifted her heavy English book from her locker. The kids up north get days off when it snows. When it's cold here, we have to go to school as usual and watch our fingers turn blue."

"Well, the cold weather is over now," Meredith predicted. "The almanac says we won't have anymore cold snaps this winter."

Kim closed her locker. "Christine, are we still planning to sleep at your house tonight?"

"As far as I know," Christine answered, taking her math book from her locker. "The house will be quiet because the little kids are going camping with my dad." She wrinkled her forehead. "Did we have math homework?"

Kim shook her head.

"Good," Christine said, smiling as she hefted her math book toward the back of her locker. "All I have to do this weekend is read that story for Mr. Cardoza. We could even read it together tonight, then we'd be free all weekend."

Meredith looked up from her locker, her book bag bulging. "Free to do what?"

Nicki noticed the load of books in Meredith's bag. "Why are you taking all those books home?" She closed her locker with a slam. "We don't have any homework except for English."

Meredith shrugged. "I like to work ahead."

Nicki sighed. "Whatever."

From her locker two rows away, Laura finally joined them. "I'm ready to go," she announced. "Are we going to walk to Christine's or should I call Mr. Peterson? It's a pretty day outside, but the wind is still a little cool."

Meredith made a face. "Honestly, Laura, we don't need your chauffeur just to take us to Christine's. We can walk there in twenty minutes. Besides, this day is positively dulcet."

"Dulcet?" asked Nicki, Kim, and Laura together.

"It means agreeable, luscious, soothing, or sweet," Meredith explained. "It's my vocabulary word for the day and I have to use it two more times in a sentence."

Nicki giggled. "Well, since we have dulcet weather, perhaps Christine has planned a dulcet evening for us?"

Christine smiled. "Absolutely the dulcet-est."

Meredith shook her head. "Vocabulary is a very serious thing. It's impossible to even think precisely unless you have the perfect word in your head." She shook her finger at her friends. "You all should learn these words along with me."

Nicki laughed. "Do we have a choice? We'll either have to learn them or carry a dictionary with us wherever we go."

Laura elbowed Kim. "Why'd you ever give her that book? We're going to feel like we're in school all the time."

Kim gave Meredith an admiring glance. "I take English words very seriously. And I would love to share a dulcet study with Meredith."

Nicki picked up her books. "Is it settled, then? Are we taking a dulcet walk to Christine's?"

"Sure," Laura answered. "Since it is such dulcet weather ou side."

"I just hope my little brothers and sister have left for their camping trip by the time we get there," Christine said. "The dulcet darlings can be a real pain."

The girls walked down the hallway and out the door, their laughter echoing in the soft winter sunshine.

━

A soft blanket of quiet lay over Christine's house when the girls arrived. Tommy wasn't home from school yet, and Stephen, Gaylyn, and Casey were off on their camping trip with Mr. Kelshaw.

"Torrie's baby-sitting until late, so she said we could use her bed," Christine said, leading the girls to her room. "We'll all be able to sleep in here if two of us don't mind sleeping bags on the floor."

"I like the floor," Kim said, stretching out on the carpet next to Gaylyn's bed.

Several baskets and a pile of fabric were heaped against the wall. "Just push all the fabric stuff out of the way," Christine told Kim. "We're still making baskets to sell and we've almost reached our goal. Torrie and I figured it will cost nearly three hundred to buy everything we need to redecorate our room."

The room was kind of mismatched, Nicki realized. She looked at the three twin beds, each against its own wall. Over Torrie's bed hung a small bulletin board on which she had tacked probably ever corsage she had ever received. The ribbons and net were still bright, but the once-colorful blossoms were brown.

Christine had a picture of Tiger Woods on the wall next to her bed, and the quilt on her mattress looked like it was at least a hundred years old. Gaylyn's bed was covered with stuffed animals, and her wall was decorated in Garfield posters. An open space lay in the center of the room, and against the only wall without a bed stood a set of bookshelves, bulging now with fabric scraps, bottles of fabric stiffener and glue, and an assortment of colored baskets.

"We all agreed to pool our money and buy matching comforters and curtains," Christine explained. "Something with roses, but they'll have to be yellow or white, not pink. With our red hair, we can't tolerate pink."

Laura laughed. "Yellow or white would be nice. You could add blue as an accent color. A soft yellow and a gentle blue would be beautiful."

Christine nodded. "I see what you mean. If we raise enough money, we're going to check on getting new carpet and maybe even wallpaper. But we'll probably just paint the walls. And we've agreed—our posters and those nasty dead flowers will come down when we redecorate. If we've got to live together, we figured we might as well make our room nice."

Meredith grinned. "The effect will be positively dulcet." She ducked as Nicki threw a pillow at her. "Come on! I've still got to use the word one more time!"

Mrs. Kelshaw stepped into the doorway. "How are you girls today?"

"Simply—"

"Absolutely—"

"Perfectly—"

"—dulcet!" they all squealed.

Mrs. Kelshaw crossed her arms. "Dulcet?"

Nicki had always thought Mrs. Kelshaw was a pretty woman. She had Christine's light red hair, but her eyes were blue and they sparkled with life. Nicki imagined that it wasn't only the six kids who created so much mayhem in the Kelshaw household . . . Mrs. Kelshaw looked like she could be as crazy as the rest of them.

"Well, if you girls need anything, just let me know. Tommy's bringing home tacos at dinnertime, if he doesn't forget, and there are snacks in the kitchen. Just remember that Torrie's coming home late, and she'll be sleeping on the couch, so keep the noise down tonight, will you?"

Christine nodded. "Okay, Mom. We will."

Mrs. Kelshaw left the room and Laura's hand went to her throat. "Tommy's bringing home tacos?" Her face had turned tomato red and her voice quivered.

"If he doesn't forget," Meredith replied. "Should we alert the media?"

"Honestly, Laura, you're not still mooning over Tommy, are you?" Nicki asked. "You haven't seen him in over a month."

"Six weeks," Laura said. "But he hasn't been out of my thoughts for a single minute."

Christine giggled. "Is that why you've been calling me more often than usual? Were you hoping he'd answer the phone?"

Laura blushed. "I always call you. I call all my friends a lot."

"But every hour?" Christine said. "I told you, Laura, Tommy has a girlfriend. He and Amy are still going strong."

Laura sniffed. "I'm not trying to break them up. I just think Tommy is incredibly—"

"Dulcet?" Kim quipped.

"No," Laura answered. "Incredibly incredible." She leaned

back on Torrie's bed and reached above her head to finger the corsages on the bulletin board. "And to think that the taco I eat tonight was touched by Tommy Kelshaw . . ." She shivered. "Doesn't that just do something to you?"

"Those tacos will be touched by the people at Taco Rice," Christine answered. "And it's very likely that Tommy will get caught up talking to his coach or Pops or Amy and forget to come home at all. We'll starve."

"Is he still working out with that Pops guy?" Nicki asked, remembering Blane Gray. "Now, *that* was a good-lookin' guy. No offense, Chris, but I think Pops is much better-looking than Tommy. There's something about those blue eyes—"

"He's solid, that's for sure," Meredith said. "His arms look like the Incredible Hulk's."

"The Incredible Who?" Kim asked.

"Forget it," Laura said. "The Hulk was some green guy on TV about a million years ago. But I don't care what you say, Nicki and Chris, I still think Tommy is the most adorable thing around."

As if on cue the front door slammed and a masculine voice called out, "Mom! I brought dinner!"

"That's him!" Laura gripped Nicki's arm so tightly it hurt.

"Okay, so let's go eat," Nicki said, trying to stand.

"I can't," Laura said, shutting her eyes. "What if I blush or faint or do something stupid?"

"It won't matter," Christine said, breezing past Laura and

Nicki on her way to the kitchen. "Tommy will be so busy burping or being gross that he won't even notice."

Four

Even Christine had to admit that Tommy was on his best behavior at dinner, but she told Nicki it was probably because he had an audience. The five girls sat at the kitchen bar while Tommy passed out tacos and drinks. Christine was the only girl not under his spell. She glared at her friends throughout dinner.

Meredith was the first to speak up. "Tommy, you look great. What have you been doing to yourself?"

Tommy reached to open a cupboard with his left hand and paused to flex his muscles. Nicki could tell that Meredith's comment had pleased him. "Oh, just the usual weightlifting," he said.

"You've really changed," Nicki added. "I can't believe how different you look even since Christmas."

Christine crinkled her nose and leaned back to look at her brother. "You really think he's changed?"

"Yes," Kim said. "He is much broader around the arms and chest."

As Meredith fizzed with laughter, Nicki bit her lip to keep from laughing and embarrassing Tommy. She wouldn't have put it in quite that way, but Kim was right.

Laura sat there in a daze, leaning her head on her hand and staring at Tommy. "Positively dulcet," she murmured at one point.

""Dulcet?" Tommy asked, holding a bottle of soda.

Laura blushed, and Meredith came to her rescue. "Good-looking," she said. "It's a compliment."

"Oh." Tommy appeared to shrug off the attention, but he left his captivated audience reluctantly, it seemed to Nicki. With no more stools at the counter, he gathered his drink and tacos and headed for the big table in the dining room.

Thank goodness. Now maybe Nicki and her friends could have a sensible conversation.

Then again, maybe not.

"I can't believe you," Meredith whispered, turning to Laura. "You turn into an absolute moron whenever a guy's around. Wake up, girl!"

Christine shrugged. "He's really not that great. If you had to live with him for a week, you'd realize it."

"He's wonderful," Laura said, nibbling her taco. She swallowed a dainty bite. "Everything's wonderful. Life is wonderful. I feel so wonderful right now . . ."

"Oh brother," Christine said, moaning. "Is she going to be like this all night?"

Nicki reached for the taco sauce. "Could be. Anything's possible."

"No, it is not." The quiet words came from Kim.

"What?"

"All things are not possible," Kim said simply.

Meredith frowned. "I suppose that is true theoretically," she said, tapping her taco shell, "but there are more possible things than one would think."

Nicki realized Kim was hinting at something. "What's not possible, Kim?"

Kim put down her taco and Nicki saw tears glistening in her eyes. "It is not possible for a Korean girl to become American. I thought I could. I learned to speak like you. I have learned to dress like you. I try to think like an American girl. But I cannot be an American girl."

"Why would you want to be American?" Christine asked. "I think it's neat that you're Korean. You came to the United States for your mother's kidney operation, right? If you're going back to Korea—"

"My parents are considering staying in the United States," Kim interrupted, "and I want to stay, very much. But first I want to be sure I can become an American girl and fit in."

Laura patted Kim's arm. "You're already as American as apple pie. Didn't you say your dad is a big football fan? And don't you love the mall?"

Kim nodded.

"Then you're as American as I am," Laura said, nodding.

Nicki rolled her eyes. "There's more to being an American than football and malls. But Kim, don't you feel at home? We've all tried to make you feel comfortable."

Kim shook her head and pointed to her hair. "Black hair," she whispered. "Black eyes. Almond eyes."

Meredith lunged over Laura to reach Kim. "Look at me," she said, pointing to herself. "Black hair, black skin, black eyes. Kim, Americans come in all shapes, sizes, and colors. You don't have to look like Nicki or Laura to be the all-American girl."

"She's right," Nicki said, stroking the silky smoothness of Kim's hair. "Americans don't look alike at all. But maybe there is something we can do to help you feel better." She looked at the other girls. "Any ideas?"

Laura shrugged. "I got her that cute sweater for Christmas. You can't get any more fashionable than that."

"She's picked up our language without any problems," Meredith pointed out. "So she doesn't need tutoring."

"Don't look at me," Christine said, lifting her hands. "Redheads with curly hair are a minority, too."

Nicki looked at Christine, biting her lip in concentration. Then an idea hit her. "Kim, would you like us to give you a perm?"

"Oh, that'd be great!" Christine said, clapping in excitement. "With Kim's long hair in tiny curls, she'll be gorgeous. We'll keep her bangs straight and perm the rest. She'll be a knockout!"

"It'd sure give stuck-up girls like Corrin Burns something to talk about at school," Meredith said. "They've been giving Kim a hard time since the beginning of the school year."

"Would you like that, Kim?" Laura asked. "Can we perm your hair tonight?"

Kim looked at Nicki for an instant, then she nodded. "Okay, let us do it!"

———

Three hours later the kitchen had been transformed into a makeshift hair salon. The smell of chemicals had sent Mrs. Kelshaw scurrying out of the kitchen, but the girls had grown used to it. Laura was painting tiny flowers on Christine's fingernails, and Meredith and Nicki had set, timed, and poured solution on Kim's tightly curled hair.

"I hope we did it right," Nicki whispered to Meredith. "I've never given a home perm before. My mom gets her hair done at a salon."

"As long as we follow the directions we should be okay," Meredith answered, reading the printed label for the tenth time. "I can't believe I poked a hole in the bottle for the neutralizer, though. I hope we didn't lose too much of the solution when it was leaking."

"I'm sure it's okay." Nicki studied the glass of milky liquid. "We only need enough to cover her head."

Laura's hand froze in midstroke over Christine's fingernail when a masculine voice sounded near her ear. "What's going on here? Sharing beauty secrets?"

Laura blushed and Christine looked up as Tommy came into the kitchen. "What do you want now?" Christine asked. "Please leave us alone."

Tommy ignored her and walked to the refrigerator. "It's my kitchen, too," he said, pulling out a gallon of milk. And it *is* a kitchen, not a salon. Whew, that stuff stinks."

He poured a glass of milk and leaned against the counter, watching the girls as he sipped from his glass. Finally, he grinned at Kim. "I think you're crazy to let these girls touch your hair."

Kim smiled, but Nicki saw a flicker of fear in her dark eyes.

"They are my friends," Kim answered. "I trust them."

"And what's this?" Tommy set his glass of milk on the counter and leaned forward to watch Laura paint Christine's fingernails. "Could you paint my fingernails, too? You could paint 'I'll get you' on my nails and it would psych out my wrestling opponents. Come on, a letter on each fingernail. Whaddya say?"

Laura only blushed and shook her head.

Tommy laughed and reached for his glass of milk. He lifted the glass to his mouth and tilted his head back.

"Stop!" Meredith screamed. "That's not milk, that's the neutralizing solution!"

Tommy spun around, his cheeks bulging, and dove for the sink, spitting and gagging. He ran the water and put his head under the faucet, allowing the water to run into his mouth and out again.

Meredith gingerly stepped over and took the glass of solution from his hand. "Excuse me," she said, "but we need the rest of this for Kim's hair."

When Tommy spun back around and looked at the girls, his normally casual expression had vanished. Nicki wouldn't have recognized him on the street, and even Christine looked at him in bewilderment. It was Tommy, no doubt about that, but nothing in that crazed face and tense body seemed at all like Tommy Kelshaw.

Tommy knotted his fist, pulled it back, and with one movement turned and sent his hand through the kitchen wall. The girls jumped and Laura let out a tiny, involuntary squeak.

Tommy turned from the wall and walked quickly past the girls and into the garage. The door between them slammed. Above the sink, a piece of shattered drywall swung back and forth, then dropped onto the counter.

Every eye turned to Christine, and she spoke for them all: "What was that about?"

Five

"I've known your brother a long time," Meredith said slowly, "but I never knew Tommy had such a temper."

"Neither did I," Christine said. "And I've lived with him my entire life. He's never done anything like that before."

Nicki walked over to the hole in the wall and peered in, but she couldn't see anything but blackness. "At least he hit an empty spot," she said. "He didn't break any of the pipes or wires inside the wall."

"My parents will have a fit," Christine said, moaning. "I'm surprised Mom didn't hear and come running in here."

"She's gone," Laura said, her wide eyes still fixed on the hole in the wall. "She told me to tell you she was going to pick Torrie up from her baby-sitting job. But she'll be back any minute."

"That sure didn't seem like Tommy," Christine said, her forehead crinkling in thought. "He's a joker, not a fighter."

"Maybe he's having trouble with someone at school," Meredith offered.

Laura jumped at the possibility. "I'm sure that's it. Tommy just couldn't be this destructive without a reason. I know it isn't in him."

"You know what they say about redheads and their tempers." Nicki lifted an eyebrow. "Besides, how do you know Tommy doesn't have that kind of anger in him?"

"I just know," Laura snapped. "I simply couldn't feel so warm

28

and fuzzy about anyone who could get that mad. Besides, Tommy's hair isn't red. It's auburn."

Christine looked at the damage. "Well, we've got a mess here. I suppose it's our fault Tommy thought the neutralizer was his glass of milk, so we should clean it up." She forced a little laugh. "After he thinks about it a while, he'll probably come in and help us clean up."

Kim picked up the biggest chunks of drywall from the counter and passed them to Christine, who buried them at the bottom of the trash can. While Nicki wiped the dust off the counter, Meredith studied the hole more closely.

"You know," she said, pointing to two pictures on the wall, "one of these pictures would completely cover that hole. We could cover the hole until your mom has time to get a repairman out here to fix the drywall."

"You'd have to move that other picture, too," Nicki said, pointing to the second picture over the sink. "Otherwise they'd be out of balance."

Meredith unhooked the two pictures from the wall and held them in their new positions. "Chris? What do you think?"

With the pictures repositioned, the hole was completely covered. "That looks fine," Christine said. "I'll get Mom's hammer and nails out of the toolbox so we can rehang them."

Kim shook her head. "But won't your mother want to know why the pictures are different?"

"Probably," Christine said, "and I'll have to tell her."

"Promise me one thing," Laura said, standing. "Let's find out what's wrong with Tommy before you turn him in. I know there has to be some reason for this strange behavior. We can ask around school and find clues and make it another mystery to solve. Please, can we do this? For Tommy's sake?"

Christine looked at Nicki. "I have to admit that I think Laura's right," she said. "This isn't like Tommy at all. I know my brother, and what we saw tonight was weird. I want to give him a chance."

Nicki looked at Meredith and Kim. "What do you think? Should we investigate and find out what's troubling Tommy?"

Meredith nodded. "I'm curious myself. It could prove to be an interesting study."

Kim nodded too, but then she pointed to the tight rods in her hair. "Please?" she asked. "Is it not time to remove them?"

"Ohmigoodness," Christine gasped. "We're ten minutes late! Get that neutralizer on her hair, fast!"

———

Kim's hair was curly, to say the least. Meredith unwrapped curls over layers of curls, curls, and more curls. Kim's eyes were as wide as her gaping mouth.

"Ohhh," she said, watching the curls unfurl. "So different."

"Is that good or bad?" Meredith whispered to Nicki. "Would she tell us if she didn't like it?"

"I doubt it," Nicki whispered back. "It was our idea and she wouldn't want to hurt our feelings. So this had better work!"

Christine took over as the resident expert on perms. "My sister Torrie's hair looked just like this when she permed hers last month," she told Kim. "Just wait until she gets home. You'll see that it looks really nice when it's all dry and combed out."

The door between the kitchen and garage opened and Mrs. Kelshaw and Torrie walked in. "Hello, girls," Mrs. Kelshaw called, glancing only briefly at the mess spread over the counters. "I'm not even going to look at my kitchen until you all are done. I'm sure you're going to clean up every bit of that mess, aren't you?"

"Yes, Mom," Christine called.

Torrie paused by the kitchen. Her gaze passed over the kitchen wall and a puzzled expression flitted over her face.

"Have a look at my nails, Torrie," Nicki said, catching the older girl's attention. "Laura's a born artist. She painted little designs on all our nails."

Torrie smiled and let out a tired yawn. "Nice. Sorry, you guys, but the Orrs' three kids have worn me out. It's midnight, I'm tired, and I'm going to bed."

"On the couch, right?" Christine reminded her. "We've got all our stuff spread out in the room."

"Yeah, yeah, the couch," Torrie answered. "The things I do for my sisters." She sighed and walked toward the family room.

Laura blew out her breath and looked at the damaged wall. "That was close. Torrie would have noticed something was different."

Nicki nodded. "She probably did notice, but she's too tired to think about it. Kim, did you see how nice your hair will look once it's combed out? But for now you should probably let it drip dry."

Kim shook her glossy wet curls and for an instant Nicki was reminded of Medusa, the mythological woman with living snakes for hair. But surely Kim's hair would be fine in the morning.

It had to be.

❤

When the sun finally peeped through the faded curtains in Christine's room, Nicki woke and tried to remember where she was. That's right—Christine's house.

After cleaning the kitchen they had gone to bed and giggled for an hour or two while they told spooky stories. Finally, they had gone to sleep.

Nicki had been awakened, though, during the night by someone—had to have been Tommy—who let the garage door slam and then closed the door of the bedroom next to theirs.

Did Tommy always keep such late hours in the garage?

She propped herself up on her elbows and looked around. Christine and Laura were still sleeping, and Nicki couldn't believe how picture-perfect Laura looked. Christine's mouth was open and she was snoring, but Laura lay flat on her back, her arms folded across her chest, as pretty as Sleeping Beauty. Her long blonde hair wasn't even rumpled.

Nicki leaned over to look at Kim, still in her sleeping bag on the floor. Kim's hair was dry and still in ringlets from the perm rods. It looked okay, and now that it wasn't glistening with water her curls didn't look so . . . alive.

Meredith had slept on the floor, too, and Nicki was surprised to see her awake and reading *More Ways to Increase Your Word Power*.

"Why are you reading that now?" Nicki whispered.

"Sleep is a waste of time once your body has sufficiently rested," Meredith replied. "Time you could spend learning something is only wasted by sleep."

Nicki fell back onto her pillow. "Oh."

"Anyway, what are you doing awake?" Meredith asked.

"Can't help it," Nicki said. "I always wake up with the sun. Mom had to put room-darkening blinds on my windows so I'd stay in bed when I was little."

Meredith nodded. "You're an early bird, and that's good. There's no need to extirpate the habit of rising early."

"Extirpate?" Nicki peered over the edge of the bed. "Is that your new word for the day?"

Meredith consulted her book. "It means to pull up by the roots,to completely eliminate or destroy. From the Latin word meaning *root*."

"Lovely." Nicki thought a moment. "Can we extirpate your habit of using big words all the time?"

"Highly unlikely." Meredith grinned. "You'd have more luck extirpating my tendency to breathe."

"Well, that's twice," Nicki said, giggling. "Quick, use it again before everyone else wakes up or you'll never hear the end of it."

Meredith put the book beneath her pillow. "You can't use the word on a whim. You have to use it in a truly proper place, not wherever or whenever you want to use it. That would defeat the purpose."

"The purpose of what?" Christine asked, rolling over and blinking her eyes."

"Go back to sleep," Nicki advised. "You really don't want to hear this."

"Sure I do," Christine croaked, her voice still husky from sleep. She glanced at Kim. "Hey, let's comb out Kim's hair. I'm dying to see what it will look like!"

"Don't wake her up," Nicki said, but she spoke too late. At the sound of her name, Kim's eyes had flown open.

Chris bounded out of bed. "Ready to see what your hair looks like, Kim?"

Kim sat up and hugged her knees. "Okay," she said, her head doing down to her knees. "Just let me sleep."

Christine grabbed a hair pick from her dresser and began to pick at the mass of curls. As she worked, the tightly wound hair bloomed into a mass of kinks.

Meredith drew her breath in sharply. "I've never seen so much hair."

"I should have started with the bottom layer," Christine said. "Now I can't even *find* the bottom layer."

"There's no way you're going to get a comb through that,"

Meredith said. "I don't think we're going to be able to brush it, either. It's too curly and thick."

"She'll just have to use a pick," Christine said, still fussing with the curls. "There, I think I've done it all. Open your eyes, Kim!"

Kim's eyes opened and she turned to look in the mirror. Behind her, Nicki, Meredith, and Christine looked, too.

Kim smiled, but her eyes were opened wide in alarm. "So different," she said, nodding slowly. "I wonder what my parents will say."

"Can't imagine," Meredith said.

Christine patted Kim's shoulder. "Don't worry. The curl will relax in a few days and then you'll be able to brush and style it like always. Until then, just enjoy the supercurly look. It's great!"

Kim cast a doubtful glance at Meredith, who smiled in assurance. "You look fine," she said. "Corrin Burns will turn green with envy."

Kim looked at Nicki next. "It's different," Nicki said, wanting to be honest. "But I think you'll get used to it. It's a whole new you."

Kim smiled at her reflection again, and Nicki knew she was trying to convince herself that the perm had been a good idea. Meanwhile, Laura slept on in her Sleeping Beauty pose, her silky golden tresses falling over her pillow without a kink.

Six

Mrs. Kelshaw called them for breakfast at eight, and Laura reluctantly woke up and pulled on her lush terry cloth robe. "Just lead me to the breakfast table," she said, walking with her eyes half-closed.

"Have it your way," Meredith said, "but I think you should know Tommy's up, too."

Laura stopped in midstep, her eyes wide. "I can't go in there like this!" she shrieked. "Y'all go on while I put on some mascara and brush my hair."

Christine giggled and led the other girls to the kitchen where a big plate of eggs and bacon waited on the bar. Tommy and Mrs. Kelshaw were in the dining room eating doughnuts and drinking coffee.

"You girls did a great job of cleaning up," Mrs. Kelshaw called. "I even like how you rearranged the pictures. I get in a rut sometimes with my decorating, so I like the change. Don't you, Tommy?"

Tommy, his mouth full of doughnut, grunted agreeably.

"You see," Christine whispered to the other girls. "I told you he wasn't always Mr. Charming."

The girls stopped talking when Tommy came into the kitchen. "You gals were quiet last night," he said, grinning. "I didn't hear a sound when I came in." He peered at Kim. "Something's different with your hair, right?" He didn't even glance at the wall where a picture now covered the hole his fist had made.

Nicki shot Meredith a puzzled look. Didn't he remember what happened last night?

Then Tommy lowered his voice and leaned across the kitchen bar. "Sorry about the wall," he said. "I lost my temper." He stood back and rubbed his knuckles. "I'll never do that again—my hand still hurts! But thanks for covering for me. I'll tell Mom and Dad and pay to have the wall fixed as soon as I get some money."

Christine peered at her brother. "Are you okay? You were acting a little strange last night."

Tommy grinned. "Never better, sis."

He opened a cupboard and took down a bottle of pills. He opened the bottle, shook out two pills, and gulped them in one easy motion.

"What's that?" Nicki asked, trying not to sound nosy.

Tommy grinned again. "Vitamins for this megabody." He winked at her. "Gotta stay in shape if I'm going to wrestle."

He put his coffee cup in the sink and grabbed a slice of bacon from the serving platter. "Gotta run," he said.

"Where are you off to in such a hurry?" Christine asked.

Tommy leaned over the counter and tweaked her nose. "If you must know, Amy and I are riding our bikes to the beach."

Just then Laura came into the kitchen, her hair brushed, her eyelashes curled, and her body clothed in a designer outfit that would have cost Nicki's dad a week's salary.

"Hello, Tommy," Laura whispered, fluttering her lashes.

"Hi," Tommy answered, stopping to let her pass. "And bye. Gotta run."

And with that, he went out the door.

—

With her voice lowered to a near whisper, Nicki addressed the other girls. "We have a new mystery to solve, remember? What was wrong with Tommy last night? How could somebody be so cheerful one minute and so violent the next?" She shuddered, remembering the stony expression and flinty fist they'd seen. What if Tommy had hit someone's face instead of the wall?

"Iron Man," Laura whispered, sliding onto a stool at the counter. "He wears Iron Man cologne."

"How do you know that?" Meredith asked.

Laura gently tapped her nose. "My nose is never wrong. Personally, I've always thought it was a little bit too big, but my mother said she'd never pay for plastic surgery because my nose is too talented. I choose all her perfumes."

Meredith held up her wrist. "Okay, Miss Nose, what perfume am I wearing?"

Laura closed her eyes and sniffed at Meredith's wrist. "You haven't put on anything this morning," she said, "but last night you were wearing an imitation of Morning Dew."

"That's incredible," Meredith said, honestly surprised.

Christine held out her wrist. "What about me?"

Laura took one sniff, then frowned. "You don't wear perfume. But you bathe with Ivory soap."

"That's really amazing," Meredith said, her mental wheels turning. "Can I use you in a science project?"

"No way." Laura laughed. "Like I said, I've always been self-conscious about my nose. Do you think it's too big?"

"It's perfect for your face," Nicki assured her.

Laura sighed and reached for a slice of bacon. "I hope so. I hope Tommy doesn't think my nose is too big. Christine, has he ever said anything about my nose?"

Christine rolled her eyes. "Right now I think he has more important things on his mind."

"Okay," Meredith said, "back to Tommy. Was last night really such a big deal? Maybe he just lost his temper. What other reason could there be?"

Nicki remembered the total lack of expression on Tommy's face as he rammed his hand into the wall. "It was creepy," she said. "He didn't even look mad. He looked more like—"

"A robot," Christine finished. "I really think something's behind this. Tommy is usually one of the calmest guys you've ever seen. My little brothers are enough to drive anyone wild, and Tommy has never lost his temper with them. His drinking that nasty neutralizer last night was nothing compared to my little brothers."

"Maybe he's having problems with his girlfriend," Laura suggested. "Maybe they had an argument and he's on his way over there right now to try to patch things up. Love can make a person do crazy things, you know."

Nicki didn't think much of that theory, but she didn't want to dash Laura's hopes. "Okay, we'll investigate his relationship with Amy," she said, mentally making a note of it. "What else could drive him crazy enough to crack a wall?"

"Maybe he's having trouble with his wrestling coach," Christine said. "I know how badly Tommy wants to do well in wrestling so Coach will put him on the varsity football team next fall. That's pretty much all Tommy cares about right now. But if things aren't going well in wrestling, he could be really upset."

"That's possible," Nicki agreed. "Okay, we'll check that out, too. Any other ideas?"

"There is something else," Kim said. "I have heard a lot about drugs since coming to this country. Is it possible that Tommy is using drugs?"

Christine's face flushed. "No way! My brother wouldn't do that!"

Nicki put her finger across her lips, reminding Christine to lower her voice. "Even if Tommy is the last person on earth who'd use drugs, that could still be a possibility," she told Christine. "Good investigators don't overlook anything."

"You don't know my brother like I do," Christine said. "We don't take drugs. My dad doesn't even like to take an aspirin unless he has a headache that's killing him. Tommy wouldn't take drugs. He's not stupid."

"Okay, so that possibility isn't likely," Nicki said calmly. "So we'll focus on our other possibilities first."

Meredith looked at Christine, who had crossed her arms and was glaring at Nicki. "We'll figure it out, so don't worry," Meredith said. "Whatever the problem is, we'll extirpate it."

Seven

"Well, the first thing investigators do is investigate the scene of the crime," Nicki explained, "although we certainly don't think there's an actual crime here."

"Okay," Christine said. "We can look around, but don't any of you breathe a word of this to anyone in my family. Tommy would kill me if he knew I was snooping in his stuff."

"We're not snooping," Meredith said. "You're just showing us through the house. So let's look at Tommy's room. We also ought to look in the garage where he keeps his weightlifting equipment."

"I'm not sure we should look through his room," Laura whispered, hanging back. "Isn't that really personal?"

Kim slipped off the stool. "Come on. I have never seen an American boy's room."

Tommy had the smallest bedroom in the Kelshaws' four-bedroom house, but at least he had the privilege of having it to himself. Nicki couldn't see anything unusual about his room. It looked like a slightly more mature version of her own little brother's room. Instead of toy cars and boats, Tommy had a football, a baseball, and a basketball scattered on the floor. Instead of *Sesame Street* posters, Tommy had posters of Bruce Lee and Dale Earnhart. And just like her little brother, Tommy had one of those basketball hoops that doubled as a dirty clothes dunk. Also like Nicki's little brother, Tommy had usually missed.

Rumpled clothes were scattered all over the floor under the basket.

Laura crinkled her nose. "Ugh, what a mess! How could such a gorgeous guy come out of this room?"

Kim's eyes were wide. "He is allowed to keep his room like this?"

Christine lifted her chin. "Not always. Mom makes him clean it up about once a week. Most of the time, though, she keeps his door closed."

Meredith was studying the room intently. "Don't touch or move anything," she said, walking by the dresser. "We need to be careful not to arouse suspicion. If Tommy has something he doesn't want us to know about, he certainly wouldn't leave it out in the open."

"Where would he leave it?" Kim asked.

"My brother hides things under the bed," Nicki said. "Once we found about twenty candy wrappers under there. He had been sneaking them and eating them in his bed."

Laura dropped to her knees before anyone could stop her. "Sorry to disappoint y'all," she called, reaching under the bed. "But there's nothing under here but a zillion dust bunnies and this."

She pulled out a fabric tape measure and held it up.

"That's my mom's," Christine said. "She was looking for it the other night, but I'll bet she never even asked Tommy. Why in the world would it be under his bed?"

"Why, indeed?" Meredith murmured, lifting a brow.

Nicki walked over to Tommy's small desk. His school books were stacked in one corner, probably untouched since Friday afternoon. On a small pad of paper someone had written, "Pops—555-3847."

Nicki tapped the pad. "Chris, is this Tommy's handwriting?"

Christine looked at the note. "Sure. And that's Pops's phone number. He and Tommy still spend a lot of time together."

Not disturbing anything in or on the desk, Nicki looked around it while the other girls peered into the closet and under piles of clothes. "There's really nothing here," Nicki said, ready to move on. Then she saw a paper that had fallen between the back of the desk and the wall. "Kim and Meredith, could you help me move this desk out a couple of inches? I need to reach something."

Meredith and Kim gently rocked the desk forward long enough for Nicki to squeeze her arm into the space and catch the paper between her fingertips.

"Got it!" She pulled the paper out and shook her head. "No wonder Tommy put this behind the desk. It's a history test, and he got a 49 on it."

"A 49?" Christine dropped her jaw. "That's impossible. History is Tommy's best subject."

She snatched the paper from Nicki's hand and looked at the long rows of questions with glaring red marks next to them. "Sorry, Nicki, but I guess you're right. Tommy must have put the paper there because Mom would have found it if he'd thrown it in the garbage."

"It could have fallen back there accidentally," Laura pointed out.

"I doubt it," Meredith said. "In order to fall accidentally, the paper would have to be lying out on the top of his books or on the desk. Would you leave that test out where anyone could see it?"

"I guess not," Laura admitted.

Meredith pointed to the top of the page. "Look at the date. He took this test just last week. Christine, have your parents said anything about Tommy failing any of his classes?"

Christine shook her head. "No, but I don't think they know about this—they'd have a fit if they did. Tommy usually gets As in history."

"I think we'd better put this back and leave it to Tommy to tell your folks," Nicki said, gently dropping the paper back into its hiding place. "In the meantime, though, we have even more proof that something is bothering Tommy. Whatever it is, it's not only making him crazy, it's hurting his grades, too."

Christine's eyes filled with tears. "This is horrible," she said. "Whatever the trouble is, I really don't want to know about it. I just want my brother to be the way he's always been."

"He's the same person," Nicki said, patting Chris's back, "but there's something wrong somewhere. We're going to find out what it is and make it right."

"I'm sure I know what it is," Laura replied. "It's that Amy Thimble."

"Trimble," Kim corrected.

"Whatever." Laura shrugged. "She's obviously making his life miserable. He needs a new girlfriend."

"We'll see about that," Nicki answered. "Now, we'd better get out of here before Torrie or Mrs. Kelshaw wonders where we went."

Nicki and the girls found it easier to check the garage. The room was full of the normal family stuff and they didn't have to be sneaky. But they found nothing unusual. Tommy's weights were in the garage, along with his belts, weight bench, and a couple of nearly empty cups from McDonald's and Burger King.

Laura removed the plastic lid and straw from one of the cups and sniffed it. "Diet Coke," she said flatly. "Nothing unusual in here."

Nicki stepped out of the garage and stood outside in the sunshine. Though it was only ten o'clock and still January, Nicki felt the warmth of the Florida sun.

"It's too beautiful a day to stay indoors," she told the others. "Why don't we walk down to Dillard's Drugstore and eat lunch at the lunch counter?"

Laura crinkled her nose. "That old place? And you want us to walk in this heat?"

"It'll do you good," Christine said. "You southern belles are too delicate. Tommy likes athletic girls."

Laura's eyes glinted. "Why, I can walk that distance any old time," she answered. "Just let me put on my walking shoes."

"There's something else we need to do," Christine said. "We need to talk to Amy Trimble. Why don't we call her and have her meet us there?"

"Isn't she riding her bike with Tommy?" Nicki asked.

"Not for much longer," Christine answered. "Tommy will be home by noon. He meets Pops here at noon every Saturday and they lift weights for a couple of hours. We could call Amy's house and leave a message for her to meet us at Dillard's."

Meredith frowned. "Do you think she'll come? After all, she doesn't know us."

Christine grinned. "If your boyfriend's sister asked you to meet her about something important, would you come?"

Meredith grinned back. "Let's make that call and start walking."

Eight

"Whew," Laura said, sliding into the biggest booth at Dillard's Drugstore. "I'm ready for a coke float. Anything cool."

"Me, too," Kim said, smiling.

Laura looked at Kim more closely. "You know, I think the curliness of your perm is beginning to loosen up. Maybe the humidity outside did it, but it's definitely less curly now. Don't you think so?"

Kim was sitting between Meredith and Nicki, and both of them turned to finger her hair.

"It's definitely looser," Meredith said.

Nicki smiled. "I could almost run a comb through it now, I think."

Kim grinned. "I think I will do something daring to celebrate, like order the spicy french fries with my hamburger."

Nicki grinned and reached for a menu. "I don't know what's come over you, Kim. You're becoming more American every day."

Kim shrugged. "That is nothing. Korean kim chee is much hotter than spicy french fries."

—

The girls were halfway through their lunch when Amy Trimble arrived. Amy's long blonde hair was windblown and her cheeks were flushed, probably because she had rushed to Dillard's to see what the girls wanted to talk about.

Now she was trying to be nonchalant and cool. After all, she was in high school.

"Hello, Amy," Christine called. "Thanks for coming. Sit down and join us."

Amy hesitated for a moment, then she slid into the booth next to Christine. Laura, who sat on Christine's other side, was momentarily squashed between Chris and the wall.

"Do y'all mind?" she asked in her sweetest southern drawl. "I'm not a bug on the wall you can squish whenever you want to." She batted her lashes in Amy's direction. "Hello, I'm Laura Cushman."

Amy nodded, then looked at Christine. "What is this about? I really ought to be home washing my hair, you know. Tommy and I are going to the mall tonight." She batted her lashes in Laura's direction.

Good grief, Nicki thought, *it's a battle between blondes.*

Christine looked at her brother's girlfriend. "I'll let Nicki explain. She's the best at explanations."

Nicki accepted the backhanded compliment and tried to think of the right words—an explanation that wouldn't upset Amy. "We've noticed that Tommy hasn't been his old self," she began. "All of us except Laura and Kim have known Tommy since we were in elementary school, and we know enough about him to notice some peculiar things." She paused. "Have you noticed anything strange?"

Amy eyed at Christine's plate. "Can I have a couple of french fries? I'm starving."

Christine pushed her plate toward Amy. "Help yourself."

Nibbling delicately on the end of a french fry, Amy shook her head. "I don't know what you mean," she said. "And I think I know Tommy better than"—she paused and looked at Laura—"anyone. We've been going together five whole months and we really love each other."

"Hasn't he seemed a little different lately?" Meredith asked.

Amy shrugged a tanned shoulder. "He's been under pressure about his wrestling, of course, but that's only to be expected. Why, I'm a nervous wreck when I'm cheering for varsity games in football season. It's perfectly normal. That's quite a big deal, you know." She smiled a little smile that seemed to say, *Of course, you don't know much because you're still in middle school.*

She swallowed the last of the french fry. "Tommy's trying so hard to get in shape for varsity football next year so we can be together. That's it, you see. He's working hard for us."

Meredith looked pointedly at Laura. Laura stuck out her tongue and crossed her eyes at Meredith, but Amy didn't notice. She dipped another french fry in ketchup and dreamily continued. "After high school we'll probably go off to college together and then get married. It's will be hard, but we're in love. We'll make it work."

"Is it possible Tommy has been feeling pressure from you?" Meredith asked. "Have you been telling him all this stuff about marriage?"

Amy blushed. "Oh no. It's an unspoken thing between

us. Some things are so obvious you don't have to put them into words."

"Are you positive you haven't been pressuring him?" Christine asked.

Amy pushed Christine's plate away. "I haven't. And I don't want you guys to get in his way, either. He's working hard for us and if that makes him a little edgy sometimes, well, that's understandable. I can put up with it, but you all don't have to."

She stood and flashed the smile that had won over the cheerleading judges. "We all want to win on this, don't we? Tommy wants to do well in wrestling so he can play varsity football. I want him to keep up the good work, so I'm not sticking my nose into anything. You all should do the same."

She smiled at Christine and then looked at Laura with a warning in her ice-blue eyes. "Bye now," she said. "Just leave Tommy alone. I can take care of him."

Nicki watched Amy walk away, then she let out a whistle. "I had no idea she and Tommy were so serious. I can't believe she's thinking about marriage."

Christine giggled. "Well, she may be, but Tommy isn't. He can barely think past his next meal. I know he isn't thinking about marriage—he doesn't even want to think about college, but my parents keep telling him he needs to plan ahead."

"I think Amy is nice," Kim said. "So pretty. Blonde hair, blue eyes—she looks like the perfect American girl."

"She is a cat," Laura snapped, "ready to pounce. I don't like her at all."

"You're just jealous," Meredith said. "She's a typical cheerleader in love with the typical football player, and you have a crush on her boyfriend."

"Did you notice what she said about Tommy?" Nicki asked. "Remember she said something about staying out of his way when he was 'edgy.' Do you think he's lost his temper in front of her like he did last night?"

"Even if he had, she wouldn't tell us," Christine said. "That girl's in love. She's more defensive of him than I am, and I'm his sister!"

A little girl came up to their table and interrupted the conversation. "Hi, Christine," she said in a soft voice.

Christine looked down. "Why, Anna, how are you? What are you doing here?"

"My mama's over there," Anna said, pointing. A pleasant-looking woman who was watching from behind a row of vitamins waved at Chris. "I'm 'posed to do this myself," Anna went on. "Would you like to buy a candy bar?"

Christine laughed and turned to the others. "Pine Grove Christian School is raising money," she said. "Anna's in the second grade and last year she sold five hundred candy bars. Right, Anna?"

Anna nodded and held out a handful of candy bars. "One dollar each," she said. "A bargain at any price."

"What an angel!" Laura reached for her purse. "Wait, I'll buy candy for everyone. Here, Anna, here's five dollars. Just give us each a candy bar."

Anna smiled and passed the candy bars around the table. She gave Christine a hug, then scampered off to her mother.

Christine passed her candy bar to Laura.

"Don't you like chocolate?" Laura asked, sniffing the wrapper of her bar. "I love the smell of cocoa butter."

"I love it, too," Christine said, "but since my dad is the principal of the school, we'll be stuck buying up whatever the kids don't sell. Last year I ate chocolate candy bars for six months. Just the sight of those wrappers makes me sick now."

Nicki wiped her fingers on her napkin. "Well, unless Amy lied to us, we know she isn't the one troubling Tommy. She's not getting in his way, and apparently they're as thick as ever."

"I'll never understand why," Laura said. "Why would a wonderful guy like Tommy go out with a cheerleader?" She pulled a compact out of her purse and powdered her nose. "Cheerleading is so sweaty."

Nine

On Monday morning, Kim met her friends at their usual spot by the lockers. She was wearing an oversized straw hat with a wide brim, and none of her hair was visible. "What's with the hat?" Christine asked.

Kim burst into tears. "All my curls fell out. Completely. Nothing is left but frizz."

Meredith lifted the hat and Kim's hair fell limply to her shoulders. "I can't believe it," Meredith said. "That was the curliest perm I've ever seen. What happened?"

"Maybe her hair is heavier than average," Nicki suggested. "Maybe we should try a perm with extra strength or something."

"It isn't good to use too many chemical things on hair," Laura warned. "My mother's hairdresser refused to color my mom's hair after she had a perm."

"Please, we must do something," Kim said, twisting her hair and covering it with her hat. "It is only frizzy now."

Nicki thought a moment. "Can we meet again tonight at your house, Christine? And Laura, do you know if there's such a thing as an extra-strength perm?"

Both girls said, "I'll check."

They simply had to do something, Nicki realized, because the school bullies weren't going to leave Kim alone. Corrin, the resident flirt of their seventh-grade class, was dying to peek under Kim's hat. She had given Kim trouble earlier in the year and it seemed that once again she wanted to cause problems.

"New hairdo, Kim?" Corrin quipped in homeroom. "Why won't you show us? It couldn't be as bad as all that, could it? Come on, take off the hat."

Kim's lower lip quivered. "No."

Michelle Vander Hagen, secure in her own position as one of the most beautiful girls in school, nodded. "I'm sure Kim is waiting for the proper moment to unveil her new do," she said, smiling. "And I, like everyone else, can't wait to see it."

Kim slid farther down in her chair.

"Cut it out, you two," Meredith snapped at Corrin and Michelle. "Kim has every right to wear a hat if she wants to."

Corrin laughed. "When's the last time you wore a hat, Meredith? Come on, nobody wears a hat unless they've got green hair or something!"

And so the rumor began that Kim Park was hiding green hair and whoever knocked her hat off and exposed the mess would be a local hero.

At lunch, Kim told Nicki she couldn't wait for school to end. Nicki couldn't help but agree. Since they had been sitting in the cafeteria, six students had come up and tried to pull Kim's hat off.

"Are you sure you don't want to take the hat off yourself?" Nicki asked. "Even though your hair is a little frizzy, at least you could prove that it isn't green."

Kim shook her head. "I will not give in to them."

Ten

Fortunately, everything worked out so the girls were able to meet at Christine's house after dinner. "I can only stay an hour," Kim told the others. "I have homework."

"I've got to baby-sit my little brother and sister tonight," Nicki said. "So we'll get this done as fast as we can. Laura, did you find an extra-strength perm?"

Laura pulled a box from her purse. "It's for hard-to-hold hair. I figure if we keep it in twice as long as it calls for, we'll have no problem. Kim will have curls that stay."

Working with the entire Kelshaw family at home was much different from working with only a couple of Kelshaws in the house. Torrie hung out in the kitchen, on the phone, of course. She spoke quietly, but the girls found they had to whisper or she'd look up and shush them.

Four-year-old Casey's squeals mixed with those of seven-year-old Stephen in the TV room next door, and Nicki found it hard to wrap Kim's hair smoothly around the curling rods. Just when she'd finally have the wiry ends of hair tucked under, a kid would screech and she'd jump and have to start over.

Gaylyn was only in fourth grade, and very curious about the older girls, so she was constantly peeping into the kitchen or manufacturing excuses to get a drink, find a snack, or put something in the trash can. Only Mr. and Mrs. Kelshaw and Tommy stayed out of the kitchen. Of course, in Laura's eyes, Tommy was the one Kelshaw who was more than welcome.

Torrie finally hung up the phone and left the kitchen. "At last," Christine said, her voice low. "Now we can talk. Where do we stand on our latest mystery? If Tommy's troubles aren't with Amy, could they be with his coach?"

"How are we supposed to find out?" Meredith asked. "We don't go to the high school and none of us has brothers or sisters who do—except Chris, of course."

Nicki thought a moment. "Scott Spence does. His older brother Nathan plays varsity football, I think. Maybe Scott could find out something for us."

"Like what?" Laura asked.

Nicki shrugged and reached for another curler. "Maybe Scott could hang around with Nathan and his friends. He could casually mention Tommy's name and ask if it's true that the coach is giving Tommy a hard time or something. The other guys would either confirm or deny it."

Christine put down the directions to the perm. "Tommy says the coach gives everyone a hard time."

"Okay, so Scott could ask if the coach is giving Tommy an especially hard time." Nicki snapped the last rod into place. "There! Now, Kim, all we have to do is squirt your head with this bottle of solution and wait."

Nicki squirted the lotion while Christine hopped down from the kitchen counter and moved toward the refrigerator.

"Anybody want a drink?"

"Sure," Laura said. "I think we're all ready to have one."

Christine grabbed a two-liter bottle of soda and poured it into five glasses, each of them decorated with tiny painted cows. Mrs. Kelshaw had been on a cow kick for a couple of years—she had even hung a huge blue cow on the kitchen wall. The blue cow hung opposite the two pictures that were now covering the hole in the wall.

Nicki watched as Kim reached for a glass and sipped her drink, careful not to budge the curlers that sprouted from her head. Laura sipped, too, like a refined southern beauty. But Christine was thirsty; she tipped her glass and gulped her drink.

Where had Nicki seen that gesture before? She closed her eyes. The other day she had been standing here next to Kim watching someone gulp a drink in just that way, in even the same kind of cow glass . . .

The realization hit her—of course! Tommy had gulped his drink in order to swallow his vitamins. For his hunk of a body, or so he had said.

She set down her glass and looked at Christine. "Does everyone in your family take vitamins?"

Christine blinked. "Sure. I mean, the little kids take those cartoon vitamins and everyone else takes one-a-days. Why?"

Nicki shrugged. "Remember the other day when we were all in here? Tommy came in and took two pills—he said they were his vitamins. But they were little white pills. They didn't look like those huge vitamins you take once a day."

Christine turned and opened a cupboard. "It's easy enough

to find out what's in here." She pulled several vitamin bottles off the shelf. "Here's the cartoon vitamins for the kids, the family's one-a-day kind, and"—she giggled—"here are the vitamins Mom takes when she's under stress." Christine looked again. "These are new. Vitamin B6—what could these be for?"

"That's the bottle Tommy had," Nicki said. "And those look like the same white pills."

"Easy to explain," Meredith said. "Tommy's a wrestler, right? Wrestlers try to build themselves up and then a day or two before a match, they try to lose water weight so they can wrestle in the lowest possible weight category."

"What does that have to do with vitamins?" Laura asked.

Meredith pointed to the brown bottle. "Vitamin B6 is a natural diuretic."

"Die-what?" Christine asked.

"Diuretic," Meredith explained. "It increases the amount of water weight your body releases."

Nicki laughed. "In other words, you have to go to the bathroom a lot more."

Meredith ignored Nicki's last statement. "Sometimes people who are trying to lose weight take B6. It's perfectly safe as long as you don't overdo it. It's not good to overdo anything."

Laura's eyes shone with concern. "Do you think Tommy is taking too many?"

"I don't know," Christine said. "He's a big boy. I don't babysit him."

"Could these pills be responsible for his mood changes?" Nicki asked.

Meredith shook her head. "That would be nearly impossible."

Nicki took the B₆ bottle from Christine, unscrewed the lid, and looked inside. The little pills looked harmless enough. And vitamin B₆ was sold in the drugstore, so it couldn't be terribly dangerous if used properly.

Laura frowned. "I don't think those little di-daggy things—"

"Diuretic," Meredith said.

"Whatever. Those things aren't what's troubling Tommy. It's that Amy. She's pressuring him too much."

"That's wishful thinking, Laura," Christine said. "He and Amy are fine. I'm with Nicki, I think we should have Scott check around with the guys in the high school to see if the coach is pressuring Tommy more than usual."

At the sound of a noise in the hall, Christine whirled around. Tommy came into the kitchen, his eyes smoldering behind an expression the girls had seen once before.

"Chris, can I see you in the garage?" he said. He grabbed her upper arm so tightly that his knuckles went white.

An expression of pain and fear crossed Christine's face, but she tried to smile. "Sure, but make it quick" she said, letting him pull her out of the room. "We've got to finish Kim's hair."

Nicki stared as the door between the kitchen and the garage clicked shut. No one said anything for a long moment.

"Did he hear us talking?" Kim whispered.

"I think he heard something," Meredith answered. "He looked upset."

"Terribly upset," Laura added, her face pale. "I wonder what he's saying to Christine."

Nicki moved closer to the door. "He isn't saying anything," she said. "It's too quiet out there. I'd better check on Chris."

She opened the door a crack and cleared her throat. "Christine!" she called, trying to sound cheery. "We need you in here to unwrap the curlers."

Not getting a response, Nicki opened the door and looked around. The family van was parked in its half of the garage, and through the van's windows she could see Tommy standing near the rack where he kept his weights. Nicki couldn't see Christine anywhere.

"Christine?" Nicki called again.

Tommy looked up, caught Nicki's eye, and then walked out of the open garage.

Nicki stepped forward and moved to the other side of the van. Finally, she saw Christine lying on the weight bench, the top of her head beneath the barbell on the stand across the end of the bench.

Nicki ran to her friend's side. Christine was crying, tears flowing freely down her face as she gasped. "Christine! What on earth?"

Christine sat up and began to cry in earnest. "He held the bar on my throat," she said between sobs. "He said to mind my own business. Honestly, Nicki, I think he could have killed me."

Nicki couldn't believe what she was hearing, but an ugly red line had appeared on Chris's throat.

"He heard what we were saying," Christine said, sobbing.

Nicki put her arm around Christine's shoulders. "We have to tell your parents. This has gone far enough."

"No!" Christine sat up and wiped the tears from her cheeks. "I don't want anyone to know, not even the other girls. They can't know Tommy tried to hurt me. Please, Nicki, please don't tell anyone. I'm fine and I'll be okay as soon as I catch my breath. I think he only wanted to scare me."

Nicki looked at the heavy barbell hanging in the stand. That heavy thing could have broken Christine's neck or damaged her throat. Whatever Tommy meant to do, he had carried it a step too far.

"Okay, Chris, I won't tell. But you have to promise me that you won't let yourself be alone with Tommy again. And we have to set a time limit on this thing—if we can't solve this mystery by the end of the week, we're telling your parents."

Christine hung her head and nodded. "Okay," she whispered, rubbing her throat. "By then, I'll tell if I have to. But I know this isn't Tommy's fault."

How could she be so sure? Christine was risking her life to protect her brother.

Suddenly, Nicki was very afraid. If Tommy did something crazy again, Nicki might not only be telling Mr. and Mrs. Kelshaw, but the police. And if Christine didn't watch her step, Nicki might be telling the story alone.

Eleven

Nicki couldn't follow Mr. Cardoza's English lesson because she was too busy thinking about what Tommy had done to Christine the night before. She still couldn't believe it was possible that quiet, easygoing Tommy had turned into a raving maniac and threatened to seriously hurt his own sister.

More incredibly, the other girls hadn't even noticed that something seemed strange when Christine and Nicki came back into the kitchen. Laura and Kim had been too involved in unwrapping the perm, though Nicki thought she caught Meredith looking at Christine a little strangely. But no one said anything else about Tommy the entire time they were together. It was as though that incredible scene had never happened.

All Meredith, Laura, and Kim could talk about this morning was Kim's hair. Laura and Meredith were gloating as if they had invented and given the world's best perm, because Kim's hair was definitely superpermed. It was curlier than it had been last time, and today it showed no signs of relaxing. Kim's hair didn't even hang down anymore. The ends of her hair stood out from her head at least six inches.

"What do you think, Corrin?" Meredith had asked Corrin Burns in homeroom. "Is that a perm or what? It's about ten times better than the one you got last summer, isn't it?"

Corrin had simply glared while Laura and Meredith giggled. At least they had found something to shut Corrin up.

But not for long. Corrin decided that anything too curly, or curlier than average, was simply weird and ought to be labeled as such.

The attack came at lunch. Corrin was sitting with Julie Anderson and Heather Linton, her two best friends. Laura and Kim walked by their table and Julie squealed. "Oh, Corrin, you're right!" she said in a voice loud enough to wake the dead. "It does look like something from Mars!"

Heather pointed at Kim's hair. "No, Julie, it looks more like she stuck her finger in a light socket."

Corrin lifted her chin as she looked Kim over. "Whatever it looks like, it certainly looks unnatural. Have you ever seen a Chinese person with an afro?"

The three girls dissolved into giggles and Kim and Laura were speechless. They hurried to join Nicki, Christine, and Meredith at their usual table.

"I saw the whole thing," Nicki said as Laura sputtered in anger. "Don't worry, Kim, those girls are just jealous. They make fun of anyone who is brave enough to try something new."

"Consider the source," Meredith told Kim. "Perpend before you react."

"Perpend?" Laura repeated. "Meredith, will you please stop using those big words that have no earthly meaning?"

"It's not a big word," Meredith answered. "It only has two syllables and it means to reflect, ponder, or think carefully."

"Then just tell the poor girl to think," Laura answered. "Better yet, tell her to ignore Corrin and her friends altogether. That would make more sense!"

"I have been thinking," Kim whispered, her eyes glistening with tears. "My parents share the same feelings that Corrin has. It is not natural for a Korean girl to have hair like this. They disapprove and said I should have asked permission. They are not prepared for a daughter with a poodlehead."

Nicki looked at Christine. She didn't know what to say.

Kim lowered her gaze. "There is another thing," she said slowly. "Tomorrow is school picture day, right? I do not want to have hair this curly for the yearbook picture. The curl is not calming down."

Nicki looked at Meredith. Kim was right. The curls looked as if they might never relax.

"Your hair is cute," Laura told Kim. "It's curly, but it's cute. You look fine."

"But I will be the only Korean in the yearbook," Kim insisted. "I will be unusual enough without looking like a freak. This is unnatural and it is not right."

Nicki shrugged. "What do you want to do?"

Kim shook her head. "What can I do? Get a haircut?"

"Then you really would look like a poodle," Laura pointed out. "Your hair is curly down to the roots. You'd have to shave your head to get rid of all the curl."

"We could straighten it," Meredith suggested. "But it wouldn't be good for your hair, especially since we just permed it yesterday. Too many chemicals aren't good for hair."

"I cannot go on like this," Kim wailed. "It was a mistake. I cannot look my parents in the eye with my hair like this."

"Okay, we'll straighten it," Nicki promised. "We'll do it this afternoon, but we've got to make time for homework, too. I don't know about you guys, but I'm falling behind in English. I didn't read my assignment last night and with my luck, we'll have a pop quiz tomorrow."

"Okay, we'll bring our homework," Meredith said. "Laura, can you get ahold of some hair straightener?"

Laura nodded. "No problem." She looked at Christine. "Can we use your kitchen again?"

Nicki's gaze met Christine's. She wouldn't blame Chris if she never wanted the girls to come over again. Last night was too bad a memory to repeat.

But Chris looked away from Nicki and pretended nothing was wrong. "Sure," she said, her voice bright. "My folks won't mind as long as we're done and have everything cleaned up by suppertime." She smiled at Nicki. "And Tommy and Torrie won't be home until dinnertime, so there will be two less people to get in our way. It'll be great to have everyone over."

Nicki was on her way to meet the other girls after school when she saw Scott Spence at his locker. "Scott," she called, "can I talk to you a minute?"

He grinned down at Nicki and, as usual, she felt a little giddy.

It was nice to have the cutest guy in school for a friend, even if other people did tease her about him.

"Your brother is on the wrestling team at Pine Grove High, right?"

Scott nodded and closed his locker. "What about it?"

Nicki tried to act as if her question were no big deal. "Does he like the coach?"

Scott shrugged. "I guess so. Why do you ask?"

Nicki hesitated. Although she trusted Scott completely, she didn't want to take any chances and have Tommy get mad at Christine if word got around that her friends were snooping. Nothing she asked Scott could get back to Tommy.

She smiled. "I heard rumors that Coach might be too tough on the guys. That he was unreasonable and he had a really bad temper. Does he?"

"I think he has a temper, but most coaches do," Scott said. "And he's also tough, but most good coaches are." Scott peered at Nicki more closely. "What's up, Nick? Are you going to go out for wrestling in high school, or are you interested in one of the guys on the team?"

"Neither," Nicki said, lifting her chin. "Just humor me, okay? Is there anything about Coach Doster your brother doesn't like?"

Scott thought a moment. "Only one thing. Nathan says that Coach plays favorites. He'll get interested in one or two guys and assign them to upperclassmen for weight training and stuff like that. My brother thinks it's not really fair that he doesn't do that for everyone. Those guys even get extra vitamins."

"Vitamins?" Nicki's nerves tensed. "Doesn't everyone take vitamin B_6 to lose water weight?"

Scott grinned. "Where'd you learn that? But no, you don't have to take B_6 to lose water weight. Simply drinking extra water will help flush out your system. Nathan just watches what he eats and drinks lots of water. Plus, he runs a couple of miles a day."

Nicki nodded. She was dying to ask if Tommy Kelshaw was one of Coach's favorites, but Scott might not know and he'd wonder why she asked. She decided to let the matter drop.

"Thanks, Scott," she said. "See you around."

Twelve

Mrs. Kelshaw and the younger kids were out by the Kelshaws' above-ground pool after school, so the girls had the kitchen to themselves for Kim's hair straightening.

Laura applied the chemical solution to Kim's mass of curls, Meredith combed it through, holding her nose the entire time, and Christine set the oven timer to buzz when twenty minutes had passed.

"What about our latest mystery?" Meredith asked, washing the smelly chemicals off her hands. "We haven't talked today about Tommy and whatever is bothering him. Has anyone come up with anything?"

Meredith was looking at Christine, who suddenly blushed. Nicki quickly spoke up. "I talked with Scott at school, but I didn't mention Tommy's name at all."

She glanced at Christine, who seemed relieved.

"I asked if there was anything about Coach Doster the wrestling guys didn't like," Nicki went on. "It seems their only complaint is that Coach plays favorites. Scott's brother, Nathan, says that Coach's favorites get assigned to an upperclassman for weight training and even get extra vitamins."

"So Tommy must be one of Coach's favorites," Laura said, wiping her hands on one of the towels that covered Kim's shoulders. "What's wrong with that?"

"Nothing," Nicki said, "except that it doesn't build much team spirit if a couple of guys are favored above the others."

"Why would being a favorite bother Tommy?" Meredith asked. "Could it be that he doesn't like the attention? Could the other guys be giving him a hard time because he's Coach's pet? Is that what's bothering him?"

Nicki shrugged. "Could be. Coming from a big family, though, I think Tommy would enjoy the special attention."

"Who are the other favorites?" Kim asked. "Perhaps they are bothered by the attention, too."

"I don't know," Nicki answered. "But I know Nathan Spence isn't one of them. We could probably find out who the coach's other favorites are by asking Pops. Maybe Coach has him training Tommy and someone else."

"When Pops comes over tonight, I'll ask him if he trains anyone else," Christine volunteered.

Just then the front door slammed and the girls heard, "Mom! We're home!"

Christine turned to her friends and whispered fiercely: "Drop the conversation! That's Torrie and Tommy. They're home early!"

Torrie came into the kitchen, her eyes dancing with excitement and her arms overflowing with bundles.

"I got it, Chris," she said, spilling her packages onto the kitchen table. "I sold two more baskets this morning and we had enough to pick up the comforters and curtains. Tommy was nice enough to go with me to the mall to help carry them. Now we'll be able to redecorate our room tonight. Isn't this stuff gorgeous?"

The girls gathered around to admire the pretty new bedding

in a soft blue background and covered with creamy yellow roses. Torrie smiled at her sister. "I don't think we can afford to wallpaper the room, Chris, but if we sell just three or four more baskets we can buy paint and a wallpaper border to match. That would be just as nice."

Christine nodded and hugged her new comforter, still wrapped in plastic. Ever since she had seen Laura's peach and cream coordinated bedroom suite, her own room (the "bar-racks," she called it) had seemed dowdy and miserable. Nicki knew Chris felt good that she and her sisters had pulled together and accomplished something.

"Mom and Gaylyn are out by the pool," Christine told Torrie. "They'll want to see, too."

Torrie grabbed a comforter and headed toward the backyard. The girls began working on their homework, except for Meredith, who checked on a strand of Kim's hair. "Almost straight," she announced.

Tommy came into the kitchen and perched on a stool next to Laura. "Hi, girl," he said, slapping the counter with his hands. "It's hard work carrying around all that stuff on a city bus. Chris, will you get me a glass of milk?"

Christine groaned, but she moved toward the refrigerator. Tommy leaned toward Laura and gave her a wink. "I'll be driving next year, you know. Then there will be no more buses for me!"

Laura laughed while Christine filled a glass. "Didn't you have wrestling practice today?" Chris asked.

Tommy took the glass. "Nope," he said. "Coach gave me the day off. When you're the undefeated champion, you're entitled to a few perks."

Tommy was obviously in a good mood, and Laura was enjoying having him around. Nicki grinned at Meredith, who was also watching the drama unfold.

Laura let out a long, exasperated sigh and looked at the empty page in front of her. "I have to write an essay and I don't know what to say," she complained, ladling on the southern accent even more than usual.

Nicki looked at Meredith and lifted a brow. Meredith nodded. Uh-huh, Meredith's look said. Here comes the damsel-in-distress routine.

Tommy leaned closer to Laura. "What's your essay about?"

Nicki closed her eyes and imagined Laura in a white gown with a pointed hat and veil, stranded on a mountaintop while Tommy raced toward her on his trusty steed. Princess Laura held out her blank notebook to the approaching knight and whispered, "My hero!" Suddenly, the picture changed and it was Nicki on the mountaintop and Scott on the horse.

Much better.

Laura's voice brought Nicki back to reality. "It's for health class—I'm supposed to write about all the reasons why we shouldn't take drugs," she said. "I know all the reasons, but I can't seem to find the words." She fluttered her lashes at Tommy. "My head is just so empty sometimes."

Tommy leaned forward on his elbows and flexed his arms. "That's easy. Our bodies are temples and we should take care of them. I don't smoke or drink, and why should I? I want to give this body the proper food and fuels to make sure it runs properly."

"Tommy won't even eat one of our unsold candy bars," Christine added. "So you know he's a health-food nut."

"But there's something else, too," Tommy added. "I'm a Christian and the Holy Spirit lives inside me. The Bible says I shouldn't do anything to my body that dishonors Christ."

Nicki wondered for a moment how someone could call himself a Christian and threaten his sister. Perhaps it was just a brother-sister squabble and she had overreacted. Or perhaps Tommy had let his temper get out of hand. Nobody's perfect, she realized, not even Christians.

Kim had been listening with interest. "Your God lives inside you?"

"Sure," Tommy answered. "That's what Jesus meant when He said He'd never leave us or forsake us. He sent the Holy Spirit to live inside us."

Nicki knew Kim and her parents were Buddhists. "What do you know about Christianity, Kim?" she asked.

Kim shook her wet head. "The Christians who came to visit when my mother was sick were kind. They said God loved us, but I never saw their God. But I saw they were filled with love. They told us one thing, though."

Kim had an amazing ability to perfectly recall anything she had ever heard, and an even more amazing ability to mimic exactly the voice she had heard speaking. More than once, her ability had enabled the girls to solve a mystery, but now Kim was remembering something for herself.

She closed her eyes and spoke in a woman's soft voice: "For God so loved the world that he gave his only Son, so that everyone who believes in him will not perish but have eternal life." Kim opened her eyes. "Does this mean something to you?"

Nicki smiled. "It certainly does!"

The kitchen timer began to buzz, and Christine shut it off. Meredith reached for the spray nozzle by the sink. While they were rinsing Kim's hair, Nicki told her Korean friend about the wonderful story of God's love for man—the story of Jesus Christ.

Thirteen

Laura had arranged a big surprise for Kim on the morning of school picture day. Mr. Peterson, her chauffeur, picked up all the girls early, then parked the limo in a quiet corner of the school parking lot. "Is this what you had in mind, Miss Laura?" he asked, his grandfatherly eyes smiling at the girls from the rearview mirror.

"Perfect, Mr. Pete," Laura answered.

Kim yawned, her long hair falling again down her back. "Why are we here so early?"

"Surprise!" Laura said. "We're giving you a makeover! I brought my hot rollers, my makeup, and my extra-large can of hairspray."

Kim's eyes widened. "Makeup?"

"Don't worry," Nicki interrupted. "Just a touch. We won't let you get out looking like a clown."

"I even brought scissors if your bangs need a trim," Laura said, digging in her nearly bottomless bag. "Have you thought of wearing your bangs a little wispier around your face?"

Kim giggled nervously. "This will be nice. Not too much, but not the old me, either."

Christine and Nicki dug through Laura's makeup bag for the right shades of lip gloss and nail polish while Laura plugged her electric curlers into an outlet in the limo.

Meredith stretched out to watch the other kids walk to

school. "This is the life, you know. We can see out, but no one can see in."

"They know it's us," Christine muttered. "Laura's the only kid who has ever come to school in a limo."

"Not always," Laura pointed out. "I usually get dropped off at the corner in your subdivision. I walk with you guys most of the time."

"And that's roughing it," Nicki said, laughing.

Laura began to wrap Kim's hair around the hot rollers.

"How's her hair holding up?" Meredith asked. "It looks straight enough, but we've put an awful lot of chemicals on it in the last few days. I'd be qualmish about doing anything else to it."

"Qualmish, huh?" Laura laughed. "Is that our word for the day?"

Meredith nodded. "It means squeamish, or that you have qualms, or second thoughts, about something."

I am qualmish about the whole idea of school today," Christine said. "Maybe we should go home."

"We're dissecting frogs in biology next week," Nicki added. "Now that's something to be qualmish about."

"I'm having qualms about having my picture taken," Kim said. "Maybe the school's only Korean girl should go home."

"Nonsense!" Laura smoothed out the last piece of hair and expertly rolled it up on a hot curler. "Now, how are we coming on her makeup? If you'll just run a light coating of Vaseline over her lashes, you'll find it lengthens them just like mascara would."

"Where'd you learn all this stuff?" Nicki asked, dipping her finger into the Vaseline. Laura was right—the Vaseline worked wonders on Kim's naturally dark lashes.

"I pick things up here and there," Laura said. She stopped and sniffed. "Does anyone smell anything strange?"

Meredith sniffed, too. "Smells like something's burning."

The girls looked back at Laura. "It's hair," Laura said, going pale. "Take those curlers out, quick!"

"That's impossible," Nicki answered, but she grabbed the nearest curler and gave the clip a tug.

The clip didn't come off; the entire curler did, with Kim's fragile hair still wrapped around it. The entire roller broke away in Nicki's hand, leaving an even, singed line where Kim's hair had been.

"Ohmigoodness!" Christine whispered. "Her hair's . . . gone!"

Kim didn't make a sound. She simply lowered her head into her hands while the other girls hurried to unwrap the hot curlers from her hair. But the chemicals from the perms and straightening had weakened Kim's hair to the point where the slightest tug simply broke her hair off. Curlers lay scattered on the floor of the limo, each one surrounded by a thick strand of beautiful black hair.

Laura began to cry. Meredith stared in horror. Christine sat quietly mumbling, "Oh no, oh no, oh no." Nicki tried to find a way to salvage what had turned out to be a fine mess, while Kim sat with her head in her hands, afraid to look up.

This wasn't a hopeless cause, Nicki decided. Although short hair was a new look for Kim, it wasn't unusual at Pine Grove Middle School.

"I know you didn't ask for this," Nicki whispered, "but lots of girls have short hair." She ran her fingers through the remaining strands of Kim's hair. "If we just comb this out—gently—and touch up the ends with some gel or hair spray, you'll have the latest style."

"I'm so sorry," Laura said, her chin still quivering, "but Nicki's right. This could be really cute, you know." She sat up and fluffed the ends of Kim's hair. "I have some styling gel here, and if you'll just let me trim the ends—"

"What choice do I have?" Kim whispered from behind her fingers. "Unless I stay here in the car all day!"

"You won't have to hide in the car." Meredith sat up straight. "We're going to fix everything, and without heat or chemicals or anything. Just relax, Kim. I know you don't feel like it now, but you've got to trust us."

—

Nicki was amazed—Kim's new hairdo was the best thing she could have done. Her hair was softly layered and something—either the boyish look or the crazy morning's events—made her look startled and slightly amazed. With her slim figure and clear skin, the new do had changed her look from pretty to cute.

"You look super," Christine assured her after Mrs. Balian took attendance in homeroom. "And Corrin and her friends aren't going to say anything. Did you see them staring at you? They like your hair!"

"You were also getting some looks from the guys' corner," Nicki pointed out. "I saw Scott and Jeff Jordan do a double take when you came into the room."

Kim blushed, and Nicki was glad that she had at least stopped crying. For a while, back in the limo, she didn't think either Kim or Laura would ever stop their tears. Laura cried because she felt guilty; Kim cried because she was shocked. She had never had short hair before.

"You're going to take a beautiful picture," Nicki assured her, knowing that school picture day was Kim's biggest worry. "And Laura was right—you should always wear that cherry lip gloss. It brightens up your whole face."

Kim smiled shyly, and Nicki was glad to see the light come back in her eyes. Laura had recovered, too, because she kept playing that smile-and-look-away-quickly game with Jeff Jordan.

"What are you doing?" Meredith interrupted. "Why do you keep casting googly eyes at Jeff?"

Laura raised her chin. "It's the fastest way I know to get a guy's attention," she whispered, grinning. "It never fails. You smile at him and look away, then catch his eye and laugh and look away, as many times as it takes until he comes over and asks what in the world you're laughing at."

"What do you say then?" Nicki asked.

Laura grinned. "You don't say anything. You just smile and

laugh again and say, 'Don't you know?' or something. In any case, he gets interested."

"He might think you have a wonderful sense of humor," Kim added.

"He'll probably just think you're crazy," Christine said. "Anybody who sits around laughing for no reason is plain nuts." She leaned toward Laura. "Does this mean you're over that crush you had on my brother?"

"No," Laura answered, "but I'm not going to cut myself off from the world's entire male population, either." She crossed her arms. "I haven't noticed any guys hanging around you all lately."

Just then Jeff walked up and leaned against the desk opposite Laura. "Hi," he said, smiling down at her.

"Hello," Laura purred.

Nicki turned away and left those two to their own conversation. Amazing, how empty-headed Laura could seem when she was trying to impress some guy. Just last night, after Tommy had left the kitchen to go lift weights, Laura had said that Tommy was the only guy in the world for her and she'd feel that way forever.

Christine had absent-mindedly rubbed the ugly red welt hidden under her collar and said, "Forget forever. Let's just get through this week."

Only Nicki had known what she meant.

Fourteen

At lunch, Nicki nibbled on a petrified chocolate chip cookie while Laura babbled about what a hit Kim's hair had been.

"Imagine!" Laura exclaimed. "Everyone's giving me credit for cutting Kim's hair! Of course, even though it was an accident, it was a good one, wasn't it, Kim?"

Kim blushed. Nicki figured she wasn't used to all the attention. Plus, she probably wasn't yet sure it had been a good accident. Her parents hadn't seen her short look yet.

Michelle Vander Hagen stopped by their table. "Laura, can you bring Kim over to our table and show us how you cut it? Taryn Myers is thinking about getting her hair cut, and she might let you do it."

Laura beamed and nearly dragged Kim out of her chair as a living mannequin.

When Laura and Kim had gone, Meredith looked at Nicki and Christine. "Will you two let me in on the secret?" she asked. "I know there's something going on between you two. If you have a reason for keeping it from Kim and Laura, that's fine. But maybe I can help."

Christine blushed to the roots of her red hair, but she said nothing. Nicki looked at her. "Can I tell Meredith? She's no dummy. She'll figure it out eventually."

Meredith lifted a brow. "Does it have anything to do with that red mark on Chris's neck two nights ago?"

81

Nicki looked at Christine again. "Told you—Meredith doesn't miss a thing."

Christine nodded as her eyes filled with tears, and Nicki took a deep breath. "Tommy went over the edge again the other night. Kim and Laura probably think there's nothing to this mystery since Tommy seemed fine last night, but two nights ago he nearly killed Christine."

Meredith leaned forward. "What do you mean, killed? Do you mean like dead killed or hurt killed?"

"Both," Nicki answered. "He was holding his barbell against her throat."

"Oh." Meredith leaned back and was quiet for a moment. "Why didn't you tell anyone else? This is serious."

Christine still didn't answer; she only looked down at her plate and stirred her food.

Nicki tried to explain: "It's embarrassing for her, okay? She loves her brother and most of the time he's okay, and it doesn't make sense, and maybe no one would believe us, or maybe people would say Christine asked for it. Tommy overheard us talking about him, remember? The worst part of it is that he could say he was only kidding or that we made it up."

"He wasn't kidding," Christine blurted out, stabbing a roll with her fork. "I've never seen Tommy like that, but he was dead serious."

"Did he say anything to you about it later?" Nicki asked.

Christine shook her head. "The next morning he teased me a little, which is his way of apologizing, but that's all."

"This is bizarre," Meredith said, stirring her milk with a straw. "I'd say he was on drugs, but last night he gave us that big speech about how his body is a temple and he would never do drugs. He sounded sincere to me. And last night he was fine, not crazy at all."

"I think he was sincere," Nicki added. "I really don't think he'd do drugs."

"Then what is his problem?" Meredith asked. "Maybe he has a brain tumor or some other disease."

Christine's eyes filled with fresh tears. "Don't even think that! That'd be horrible!"

Nicki shushed her. "If it is some medical problem, wouldn't you want to know about it in time for the doctors to help you?"

Christine shook her head. "I don't think it's anything like that. Tommy just had a physical exam before wrestling season. The doctor said he was in perfect health."

"Well, maybe it's something that just started," Meredith suggested. "I don't know much about brain tumors, but I could do some research on the Internet."

"You should know that we've decided to keep that story to ourselves until the end of the week," Nicki said. "Christine doesn't want to tell on Tommy, but if things don't get better by the weekend, she promised to tell her parents. She can't take any chances if either her life or Tommy's is at stake."

Meredith nodded. "Okay. I'll read up on a few things to see if I can help. Maybe it was some crazy thing and he's better now. He certainly seemed okay last night, didn't he?"

Nicki grinned. "Okay enough to make Laura fall in love with him all over again."

"Is there anything else we should investigate?" Meredith asked.

Nicki paused. "We really don't know what to do. Chris and I were going to check out the wrestling team's practice this afternoon to learn more about Coach Doster. Chris is keeping an eye on Tommy while he's at home, too. What else can we do?"

Meredith pressed her lips together. "It's just an idea, and it may be crazy, but Christine, can you bring me one of Tommy's vitamins?"

Christine raised a brow. "Why? You can buy vitamin B₆ at any drugstore."

"I want one of Tommy's. Can you get it for me without his knowing that you're taking it?"

Christine nodded. "I'll bring one tomorrow."

After school, Laura and Mr. Peterson drove Kim home. Kim had wanted Laura to be with her when she showed her new haircut to her folks. Nicki couldn't blame Kim for wanting moral support. Mr. and Mrs. Park seemed to like Nicki and the rest of Kim's friends, but Nicki was sure they wondered what was happening to their daughter. Kim's hair had gone from straight to curly to frizzy to supercurly. And now—a short-short haircut?

Laura had better stay long enough to assure the Parks they weren't completely crazy.

Nicki walked by the library and waved at Meredith, who was preparing to spend a couple of hours surfing the Internet. Nicki was glad Meredith enjoyed that kind of thing—she'd be positively qualmish at the thought of spending an afternoon reading medical Web sites.

Christine and Scott were waiting for her by the flagpole in front of the school. "Scott, I'm glad you got my note," Nicki said, smiling. "Would you mind going with us this afternoon? Chris wants to see her brother practice, but we don't really know our way around the high school. We're afraid we'll look stupid wandering around in the wrong places."

Scott stood a little taller. "Sure, I'll go with you. I've gone there with Nathan lots of times. Besides"—he grinned—"I like to watch the cheerleaders practice."

When Scott, Christine, and Nicki walked into Pine Grove High's gym, the guys on the wrestling team were doing stretching exercises. Nathan noticed his brother and nodded. Tommy looked up and quickly looked away.

"He doesn't look so happy to see us," Nicki whispered as they found a seat in the bleachers.

"No," Christine said. "He doesn't."

The varsity cheerleading squad was practicing at the far end of the gym, and Nicki easily picked out Tommy's lively blonde girlfriend. "How's Amy these days?" she asked Christine.

"Amy Trimble?" Scott answered, looking in the girl's direction. "I'd say she's really fine."

Nicki rolled her eyes and was surprised to feel a twinge of jealousy. Scott was kidding, she knew, but still, Nicki was brunette, tall, and gangly, nothing like the petite, blue-eyed bundle of Amy.

They sat and watched wrestling practice for an hour. At one end of the gym, the girls cheered, squealed, and dissolved into giggles whenever someone did the wrong kick or messed up a move. At the other end, Coach Doster barked orders to the guys who were practicing moves on each other on the practice mats. Nicki decided that Coach looked like a bulldog. He had brown beady eyes, large, pouchy cheeks, and a double chin. If he had a studded leather collar around his neck, the picture would be perfect.

The wrestlers were nothing like dogs, though, Nicki decided. They were more like cats. Long, lean, and smooth in their movements, they slipped and moved and pounced on their opponents. They couldn't all practice at once, so when the wrestlers weren't on the practice mats, they moved around the gym, stretching, getting long drinks of water, or running up and down the bleachers. Not once did Tommy glance at his sister and her friends. Nicki noticed that he also never looked toward Amy. He seemed totally wrapped up in his wrestling.

When Coach Doster called for Tommy and Nathan to have a practice match, Nicki, Scott, and Christine sat a little straighter. Maybe now things would get exciting. But Tommy, moving like a panther, had Nathan pinned in ten seconds.

Scott seemed a little embarrassed, but he managed to laugh. "I don't know what's gotten into your brother, Christine," he said, "but he's gone from mediocre to machine in just a few weeks. He's incredible."

"He lifts weights," Christine said in a bored voice. "All the time."

Scott whistled. "Nathan lifts weights, too, and has been lifting for the past year. But he's not anything like Tommy—at least, not yet."

Nicki watched as Tommy stood up, offered a hand to Nathan, and then stretched confidently. He walked over to Coach and gave him a pat on the back. The Bulldog grinned at Tommy, then jerked his thumb toward the south side of the bleachers.

What was at the end of the bleachers? As Nicki watched, Tommy disappeared behind the rows of seats.

"Where is the girls' rest room?" she asked Christine. "Can I get there by going through the girls' locker room?"

Christine nodded. "I would think so."

"I'll be right back," Nicki promised. She climbed down the bleachers, turned toward the girls' locker room, and, when no one was looking, dove under the north side of the bleachers.

Down at the far end of the seats, through the maze of metal supports, Nicki could see Tommy and Pops Gray. Pops was holding out a brown bag and explaining something Tommy apparently didn't want to hear. Tommy had both hands on his hips and looked exasperated. He raised his hands, but Pops kept smiling. He caught Tommy's hand, placed the bag in it, and patted him on the shoulder. But before leaving, Pops turned and pointed once again to Tommy and said something that made Tommy frown.

What happened next made no sense to Nicki. Creeping through the maze of metal under the bleachers, she crept close enough to see Tommy walk toward the locker room with the brown bag. He paused in front of a trash can, though, and hesitated, mindlessly tapping the bag against his palm. After a moment, Tommy brought his right fist down on the heavy plastic lid with such force he dented the can. The crashing noise was nearly swallowed up in the hubbub of the gym, and the few people who did turn to look merely saw Tommy walking with his usual macho swagger, as if nothing had happened. After that, Tommy walked into the men's locker room, and Nicki was more confused than ever.

Fifteen

The next morning brought surprises. As usual, Laura's chauffeur dropped her off at the corner in the subdivision where Nicki, Meredith, and Christine lived, and they walked to school together. Kim rode bus 33, which picked up all the kids from Levitt Park Apartments. The bus usually arrived at 8:27 and Kim was always at her locker by 8:30.

But on this Thursday morning, Kim was nowhere in sight.

Meredith looked at her watch. "That's strange. You can usually set your clock by Kim."

Christine looked worried. "Maybe she's upset about her hair."

"That couldn't be," Laura said. "When we took her home yesterday, she liked it."

"What did her parents say?" Nicki asked.

Laura shrugged. "They were polite, as always, and said she looked fine. I don't think they care what she does with her hair—they just want her to be happy and fit in. Mrs. Park asked me if it was acceptable for an American girl to have such short hair, and I said yes."

Christine was still concerned. "I hope she's not sick or something. Come on, let's get to homeroom early so we can talk. There's a new development I want to tell you about."

The girls were floored when they opened the door to homeroom and saw Kim sitting at her desk. At least, Nicki thought, the girl there looked a little like Kim.

"Surprise! What do you think?" the dark-haired girl asked with a smile.

"Ohmigoodness," Christine said. "What have you done?"

"What did you do?" Meredith asked. "Watch MTV all night?"

Kim's hair, which had beautiful soft waves yesterday, now stood on end, held in place by a glittery gel. She wore blue mascara, silver eye shadow, and lipstick so red it had begun to stain her teeth. Two purple blotches marked the top of her cheekbones, and from her ear dangled a blue plastic Smurf with a noose around his neck.

"When did you pierce your ears?" Nicki asked, fascinated that so sudden a change could happen in such a short time.

"I didn't." Kim turned her head so Nicki could see a large paperclip holding the Smurf to Kim's ear. "I improvised."

Laura had gone pale with shock, but Christine clapped her hand over her mouth to stifle a giggle. Nicki stood and stared in fascination while Meredith sat down and shook her head.

"Where did you get this idea, Kim?" Meredith asked. "What magazine did you copy? *Seventeen? Sassy? Rolling Stone?*"

Kim pulled out a copy of *Teen Model*. "Here it says I should find my style and be true to it no matter what my friends do or say," she said. "It also suggested following one's heart to the extreme."

"That's one word for it," Laura muttered, falling ungracefully into her chair. "Extreme."

"Did it say to hang a Smurf from your ear?" Christine asked. "Or would one of the seven dwarfs work as well?"

Kim refused to be embarrassed. "The article said you should not be afraid to advertise the things you like," she said. "And I like the Smurfs."

Nicki slid into her desk and lowered her head. Never had their group undertaken an experiment that had failed so miserably. They had tried to make Kim feel like an American girl, but the young lady with them looked more like an American weirdo.

"I would have worn the clothes on this model, too," Kim said, pointing to a girl dressed in heavy-metal leather and chains, "but I do not own anything like this."

Laura shook her head. "Honestly, Kim, haven't you learned anything about America yet? What we look like says who we are, and what we should be is gentle, refined, and cultured."

"Not necessarily," Meredith interrupted. "While you may prefer cashmere sweaters and tennis clothes, Laura, the rest of us don't. I like the hip look."

"I don't have a choice," Christine said, shrugging. "I wear whatever my sister outgrows, so I'm just me. You can't always judge a person by what she looks like."

"Sometimes you can," Nicki pointed out, looking at Kim. "And Kim, right now what you're wearing says you're a mixed-up girl. Your head is saying radical and your clothes are saying traditional. I have no idea what the Smurf is saying. If you know what's good for you, you'll trust me and take off the Smurf."

"Might be a good idea to go with us to the rest room to wash some of that goop off your hair and face," Laura said.

Meredith stood up. "I'd hurry, if I were you. Remember the hard time Corrin and Michelle gave you when you wore a hat? That day will seem like a picnic if you let them see you like this."

"I'll ask Mrs. Balian for permission so we can be late," Christine said.

"And I'll stand outside and try to keep Corrin and Michelle away from you until you look like yourself," Nicki said. "Kim, you go with Meredith and Laura. Trust me. Made up like this, you're not being true to yourself—you're only being true to a magazine. You'll feel better in a few minutes."

When Meredith, Laura, and Kim came back into homeroom after the bell had rung, a few people looked curiously at Kim's wet hair, but no one said anything. Nicki breathed a sigh of relief. Kim was trying so hard to be the American girl that she had forgotten to be herself.

"That's much better," Nicki said when Kim sat back down. "With your pretty features, you don't even need makeup. And the good thing about short hair is that it'll be dry in just a few minutes."

Kim gave a little nod and pulled out a book.

"We may have hurt her feelings," Laura whispered to Nicki. "She really thought she was doing a good thing. She swallowed that article in the magazine as gospel truth."

"But we did the right thing," Nicki whispered back. "She'd have been crushed if Corrin and those other girls had seen her."

Meredith pulled out a sheet of notebook paper and passed it to Nicki. "I worked all afternoon in the library," she said, "and I really don't think that problem we discussed"—she nodded toward Christine—"is medically related. Although if it continues, another physical exam would be a good idea."

"Thanks." Nicki glanced at Meredith's complicated notes and handed the paper back to her. "I'll take your word for it."

Nicki looked back at Christine to see if she had heard Meredith, but Christine's head was down on her desk. "Christine!" Nicki whispered. "Wasn't there something you wanted to talk to us about?"

Christine lifted her head. "It's nothing," she mumbled, then she shook her head. "It's a family problem. Dad had all that money from the candy sale at our house and this morning he said fifty dollars was missing. He thinks Torrie and I took it."

Laura gasped. "Why would he think that?"

"Because we bought all that stuff for our room," Christine answered. "He thinks we took the money because we got impatient trying to earn it. Torrie tried to prove that we had earned every penny by selling baskets, but I don't think Dad believed her."

"Maybe someone else took it," Meredith suggested. "Maybe one of the little kids who didn't realize what it was for."

Christine shook her head. "Dad keeps the money in a special cashbox on a high shelf in the kitchen. Only Mom and Dad, Torrie, Tommy, and I even know it's up there. Gaylyn might know, but she couldn't reach it. But the thing that makes us look guilty is that no one else needed that much money. Fifty dollars is a lot."

She put her head back down on her desk. "I'll probably be grounded for the rest of my life. And my allowance will be cut off until I'm thirty. Oh yeah." She sat up and reached in her purse. "I got that vitamin you wanted, Meredith. Tommy nearly caught me, too. I was scared to death."

Christine opened the change purse of her wallet and fished out a small white pill. Meredith took it and held it up to the light. "How'd you get it?"

Christine shrugged. "After dinner, everyone in my family watched *Andy Griffith* reruns. I snuck into the kitchen and got a vitamin and stuck it in my pocket, but as I was leaving the kitchen I bumped into Tommy." She laughed. "I think I scared him as badly as he scared me."

Nicki thought a minute. "Does everyone in your family watch *Andy Griffith*?"

Christine nodded. "Unless Torrie's talking on the phone. And except for Tommy, who lifts weight after dinner."

Meredith had obviously been following Nicki's thoughts. "Chris, do you think Tommy could have taken the fifty dollars? He was sneaking into the kitchen last night when he thought you would be watching TV."

Christine laughed. "No way," she said, then her eyes grew serious. "I mean, I don't think so. I know the old Tommy would never steal from Dad, but do you think it's possible now?" She looked at the other girls, worry showing in her eyes. "Oh no. If he didn't take it and he saw me sneaking around, he probably thinks I took the money!"

Laura patted Christine's arm. "I'm sure nobody took it. You're not a thief and neither is your brother. Your dad probably misplaced the money, that's all. He'll find it tonight and everything will be fine."

"That reminds me," Christine said. "Tonight is the last wrestling meet of the season. Tommy's been undefeated so far and if his team wins tonight they'll go on to the state championship. Our whole family is going and I'd love it if you guys would come, too."

"I can't," Meredith said. "I'm going to be doing some work with a friend of my mom's at the university lab."

"I cannot, either," Kim said, ducking her head. "I am behind in my studies." She blushed. "I have been reading too many magazines."

"I'll go with you," Laura said. "I think wrestling is horrible, but since it's for Tommy, I'll go."

"It's not like the wrestling you see on TV, Laura," Nicki said. "And I'd like to go, too, Chris. Who knows? Maybe Scott will be there, too."

Sixteen

The gym was more crowded than Nicki could believe. Wrestling wasn't exactly a popular sport at Pine Grove High, but the team had done exceptionally well for the last two years and the fans were appreciative.

Scott caught Nicki's eye and came over to where she, Christine, and Laura stood at the bottom of the bleachers. "Can I sit with you guys?" he asked.

Laura batted her lashes at him. "We're not guys, we're girls," she said, "but you can join us."

Nicki rolled her eyes. "Let's sit down front, okay? We can see better from there."

They found seats right in front of the center mat. "The view here is great," Nicki said as they sat down. She turned to Scott. "Is Nathan wrestling tonight?"

Scott nodded. "He almost didn't make weight because he has to wrestle in the division right below Tommy. The coach wanted to use Tommy, so Nathan had to work off a few pounds so he could wrestle in the lower weight category."

Nicki nodded. Was this another example of the way Coach Doster played favorites?

The two teams came out and seated themselves in two rows of chairs that faced each other. The mat lay in between them like a ceremonial proving ground, and Nicki began to feel nervous for the first two contestants. They were the lightest wrestlers, both freshmen, and Nicki felt sorry for the loser when he was pinned in less than a minute.

"Coach Doster certainly knows what he's doing," Scott told her. "That was a great move. If we keep this up, we'll skunk this other team."

Nicki nodded, but the arrival of Pops Gray drew her attention. Pops walked in and caused a visible stir among the female spectators. As an unofficial team trainer, Pops walked down the line of Pine Grove wrestlers, giving high-fives and patting shoulders. But Nicki noticed that when Pops passed Tommy, Tommy didn't even look up. Pops paused a moment, then smiled and deliberately stepped on Tommy's foot in its thin wrestling shoe.

Tommy flinched, but he never met Pops's eyes. Nicki watched, fascinated, as Pops went on walking down the line while Tommy's face reddened in silent fury.

Seventeen

Nicki leaned forward, watching the guys. Why had Tommy ignored Pops? And why in the world had Pops deliberately stepped on Tommy's foot?

She looked at her friends, but Scott, Chris, Laura hadn't noticed. Laura was busy glaring at Amy Trimble, who sat several feet away with her friends. The varsity cheerleaders didn't cheer at wrestling meets, so tonight Amy was cheering privately for Tommy. Scott was watching his brother as Nathan warmed up for his round, and Christine gloomily studied the crowd.

The next match was between Nathan and a tall, skinny guy from the opposing school. It was interesting to watch them grapple for the best holds, but Nicki really didn't understand much about high school wrestling. She had to admit that the outrageous professional wrestling on television was more entertaining. Her grandmother was practically addicted to it.

As the high school athletes wrestled, Nicki leaned toward Scott. "So does your brother like Coach Doster any better these days?"

Scott snorted. "Why should he? He still plays favorites, like always. But Nathan said he finally figured it out. It's the guys who'll be playing football in the fall who get all the special attention."

"Doesn't Nathan like football?"

"He's more into track and wrestling," Scott answered. "He

likes sports where you have to think at least a little. He says all a linebacker has to do is get out there and fall down on someone."

Nicki laughed, then sighed in relief as the referee held up Nathan's arm at the buzzer. Nathan won his match on points.

While Scott stood and clapped for his brother, Laura turned to Nicki. "Honestly, it doesn't make a bit of sense to me," she said. "And don't you think they look a little silly in those tights and Superman shoes?"

Nicki grinned.

"And now, wrestling in the 142-pound class," the announcer intoned, "is Tommy Kelshaw for Pine Grove High. His opponent from Lake Tarpon is Richie Stevens."

Tommy slipped his letter jacket from his shoulders and walked over to the coach. Nicki noticed that Laura was not bored now. In fact, her hands were actually trembling. Amy had perked up, too.

"Come on, Money!" a familiar voice called from the crowd.

Christine blushed. "My dad," she whispered. "He's passed his old nickname on to Tommy."

Tommy's friends had another name for him. "Ter-mi-na-tor!" they chanted, getting louder and faster. "Terminator! Terminator! Terminator!"

Tommy didn't seem to hear them, though, and he went through the motions of shaking out his arms and legs before he crouched down to face his opponent.

The referee blew his whistle and stepped out of the way. Richie Stevens made a catlike move that tripped Tommy, but Tommy caught himself and regained his balance without falling. He did, however, step out of the circular boundary, and the referee blew his whistle.

The next few seconds seemed to unfurl in slow motion. The referee pointed to the place on the mat where Tommy was supposed to kneel, but Tommy spun around. Instead of kneeling on the mat, he reached toward Richie with his left hand and caught Richie's dark hair. Tommy's right fist rammed Richie's nose.

Nicki heard a crunch and a collective gasp from the crowd. Blood spurted from Richie's face while the referee blew his whistle.

Laura, Nicki, and Scott stared in astonishment.

"You're outta here!" the ref roared at Tommy, but Christine's brother had turned and was already running out of the gym.

Laura looked at Nicki. "What on earth?"

Christine shook her head. "We should have said something, Nicki," she said, tears filling her eyes. "We should have said something days ago."

Richie Stevens lay on the mat while his coach held a blood-soaked towel over his face. A man from Lake Tarpon's crowd stood up and yelled, "We're gonna sue! We're gonna sue that punk Kelshaw kid, Pine Grove High School, Coach Doster, and you, you stinkin' ref!"

Coach Doster stood to the side, his hands open helplessly. He looked toward Pops Gray, who shrugged, then Coach jerked his head toward the door. In the midst of the confusion, Nicki saw Pops Gray slip out of the gym.

Another wrestler from the Lake Tarpon team lunged at Nathan, who was watching in bewilderment, and suddenly the two teams erupted into a brawl. Whistles blew and punches flew, but the one who had started this mess was nowhere to be seen.

Christine moaned. "I can't believe Tommy started this. Look at my parents! They can't believe it, either."

Nicki glanced up to where Mr. and Mrs. Kelshaw and the little Kelshaws sat in a row. Tommy's mother sat upright, her fingers tightly curled around the shoulder strap of her purse. Even four-year-old Casey was silent for once, and so were Stephen and Gaylyn.

The announcer repeatedly asked for order, and after the scuffling subsided, the entire gym finally stilled.

"Due to unsportsmanlike conduct on the part of the Pine Grove team," the announcer said, "this match is forfeited to Lake Tarpon High. The Lake Tarpon High School athletes will advance to the state championship."

The cheering Lake Tarpon team filed out quickly, waving their fists at the stunned Pine Grove crowd. The bleachers erupted in noise and confusion. Tommy's teammates surrounded Coach Doster, and Nicki could hear snatches of angry words: "They can't do that, can they?" "All because of one guy?" "What about the rest of us?" "That was a cheap shot, man."

Nathan said nothing, but stood in silence apart from the

team. He had worked hard and won his match, but thanks to Tommy, he now had a black eye and everything was lost. Nicki saw Nathan glance over at Scott, and Scott's jaw tightened as the brothers' eyes met.

"Where did he go?" Scott asked, turning to Christine. "Where did Tommy run? And what made him hit that guy?"

"We don't know the whole story," Laura said. "Maybe that Richie guy said something ugly. Or maybe he did something we couldn't see."

But Nicki and Christine realized the anger they had seen was nothing new for Tommy. They had seen it before in the kitchen. Christine had seen it when Tommy threatened her with the barbell, and Nicki had seen him hit and dent a trash can without even flinching. Nicki also knew that Tommy had been angry before the match began. Something had happened between Tommy and Pops.

"Laura," Nicki asked, "can you call Mr. Peterson? I think we need to go someplace."

Laura nodded. "Where are we going?"

"I don't know yet, but I will soon," Nicki answered. "Will you call him to pick us up?"

Laura pulled her cell phone from her purse and Nicki turned to Christine. "Will your parents mind if you come with us?"

Christine shook her head. "They'll be glad to have one less kid to worry about. I'll let them know Mr. Peterson will bring me home."

Scott looked at Nicki. "What's my job?" he asked. "You've given everyone else something to do."

Nicki smiled. "Your job, if you decide to accept it, is to point out any guy on the wrestling team who is one of Coach's favorites."

Scott's smile faded. "You're kidding."

"I'm not. I need some information, and I think only one of Coach's favorites can give it to me."

Scott looked toward the mat, where the angry athletes were still milling around. "Okay—see the tall guy with dark hair? That's Jared Lewis. Nathan says he's being trained by Pops Gray, too."

"Thanks, Scott." Nicki smiled and stood. "See you tomorrow in school. I'll let you know how everything turns out."

Scott turned and watched her walk away. "Hey, Nicki," he called after her and the other girls, "you'd better be careful."

Eighteen

Nicki didn't know how to approach Jared Lewis. He was in high school and she was only in seventh grade . . . but she had one idea, thanks to Laura.

She deliberately walked across Jared's path and caught his eye. She giggled, looked away, and casually strolled to the water fountain.

She felt like a total idiot as she bent for a drink of water. None of these guys would be in the mood for flirting.

But when she straightened up, Jared was watching her. She smiled at him as if they shared a secret.

She pulled a wisp of hair from her face as she bent to take another drink. One more time and she'd try the direct approach.

When she lifted her head this time, Jared Lewis stood behind her.

"Do I know you?" he asked. "Are you somebody's little sister?"

Nicki wanted the earth to swallow her whole, but she forced a smile and remembered everything her mother had ever said about being confident. "No, I'm not," she replied. "I'm somebody's older sister."

"Oh," Jared said. When she moved out of the way, he leaned to get a drink from the water fountain himself.

He was going to lose interest unless she acted fast. To avoid losing him, she said, "We have friends in common."

"We do?" Jared straightened and wiped his mouth with the back of his hand. He wasn't even sweaty, because he never had the chance to wrestle, but he looked like Tommy: strong, muscular, and sculpted. Laura would faint dead away and even Christine would be struck speechless, Nicki realized, but she pressed on.

"Yes," she said. "I know Pops Gray, too. In fact, I was supposed to go to his house tonight and pick up some vitamins for Tommy."

Jared smiled. "That's right, I saw you in the stands with Tommy's sister. Do you need a ride or something?"

Nicki shook her head. "I have a ride. But I've never been to Pops's house and I lost the address."

"Easy," Jared answered. "The last house on Archer Lane. Pops will be in the shed in back, probably. But you'd better take the money Tommy owes him, or you'll never get the stuff."

Nicki's eyes widened. What money? But she caught herself and shrugged. "No problem. Thanks, Jared."

—

Christine and Laura were waiting for Nicki as she walked up. "Perfect timing!" Laura said, pointing to the long black limo that had just pulled up. "But where are we going?"

"To the last house on Archer Lane," Nicki said, climbing into the backseat. "Hello, Mr. Peterson."

Christine climbed in behind her. "Who lives on Archer Lane?"

"Pops Gray."

Laura closed the door. "Why are we going to his house?"

"Because we're going to find out once and for all why he's called Pops," Nicki said. "And because I think Tommy is there."

The car began to pull out of the school parking lot, then Mr. Peterson braked to a stop. "Laura," he called, "isn't that your friend?"

The girls looked out the window in time to see Meredith running after them. Laura leaned over and opened the door for her.

Meredith was breathless when she climbed into the backseat. "I thought I'd meet you guys here," she explained. "Why is the wrestling match over so soon? I couldn't believe it when I walked up and saw the limo pulling away."

"Pine Grove had to forfeit," Christine explained, "because my brother smashed a guy's nose."

"What?"

"It was terrible," Laura said. "But I'm sure Tommy had a reason for doing what he did."

Meredith nodded, a glint in her eye. "He had a reason, all right. Here it is." She pulled a small plastic bag out of her purse. In it was half of a small white pill.

"What's that?" Laura asked.

"Is that Tommy's vitamin?" Christine asked. "The one I got for you?"

"It's the pill you brought me," Meredith answered, "but it's not vitamin B_6. I had it tested at the university lab. This is Dianabol."

Christine shook her head. "I don't get it."

"It's an anabolic steroid," Meredith explained. "And this explains why Tommy has been acting so weird. He's been taking drugs and he may not have even known it."

—

While the car slipped through the darkness to Archer Lane, Meredith tried to explain what steroids do to athletes. "Steroids build muscle quickly, but too quickly. They can cause dangerous side effects, including acne, balding, damage to the heart and kidneys and they upset hormone production. Plus, for a kid as young as Tommy, bone growth can be stunted." Meredith shook her head. "If he ever wanted to grow taller, he's certainly doing the wrong things."

"So it's the pills that have been making my brother wacko?" Christine asked. "They created the teenage terminator?"

"They induce what are known as 'roid rages,'" Meredith said. "They would also explain why his grades have been slipping. His brain has begun to revolve around his muscles and everything else has taken a backseat."

"I can't believe Tommy would do this," Christine said, looking at her hands. "I mean, he's a Christian and you all heard what he said about not messing up his body. It goes against everything we believe in."

Nicki spoke up. "I don't think he knew what he was doing." She told the others about seeing Pops and Tommy together, and how Pops gave a package to Tommy and obviously wanted something for it. "And tonight, Jared Lewis told me that Pops wanted the money Tommy owed him before he'd get anymore stuff."

"So Tommy really thought they were vitamins?" Christine asked, her voice breaking.

Nicki nodded. "Looks like that. Maybe Pops gets everyone mentally and physically hooked on steroids before he starts charging them and tells them what they've been taking. I also think Coach Doster encourages Pops to give steroids to the guys he wants on his football team."

"So they both win," Laura whispered. "Pops gets his money and Doster gets a championship football team."

"But the guys get hurt," Meredith whispered. "And most of them don't even know it."

—

It wasn't far to Archer Lane, and Nicki realized Tommy could easily have traveled there on foot. A dented TransAm was parked in the driveway of the last house, but the place looked deserted.

"That's Pops's car," Christine said, pointing to the TransAm. "He's here."

Nicki asked Mr. Peterson to park across the street and turn the limo's lights off.

"Are you girls sure you know what you're doing?" he asked, turning to look at them. "Laura, I'm not sure your mother would approve of this."

"It's okay," Laura assured him. "We'll stick together, and if we're not back in ten minutes, you can come get us."

"Jared said Pops would be in the shed," Nicki reminded them. "Let's go peek and see. If Tommy's there, we'll try to talk to him. If not, we'll leave."

The four girls slipped out of the car and quietly closed the limo's heavy door. No streetlights lit this end of the road, but through the vague light of the moon they could see the outline of the house and a tree in the side yard. They tiptoed through the grass, already wet with evening dew, and Nicki found that somehow she had been given the front position.

They paused under the tree. Nicki tried to give her eyes time to adjust to the gloom.

"Tommy's been here," Laura whispered. "I smell Iron Man cologne."

Nicki took a deep breath. "Okay, then. Let's go up to the side of the shed. That way we can hear without having to cross the door. We don't know if someone might come out suddenly."

Meredith, Laura, and Christine nodded, their eyes wide in the light of the moon. They followed, single file, as Nicki crept toward the side of the utility shed.

A light burned in the shed, and it poured out across the lawn through a half-open door. Nicki avoided the light, walking toward the other, darker side, but when a hand suddenly gripped the sliding door and opened it wider, she froze with her heart in her throat.

With a burst of nervous energy, she dove to the safety of the windowless side of the shed. As the others glided into place behind her, she put her finger across her lips and knelt to listen.

"It's too hot in here," a guy said.

Another male voice answered: "It's too hot everywhere after

your brilliant move. I hope you're not planning on hiding out here until everything calms down. You'll be here for weeks."

Nicki didn't need Christine to tell her they were listening to Tommy Kelshaw and Pops Gray.

Nineteen

The girls crouched in the darkness and listened. "Man, I don't know what came over me," Tommy said. "Suddenly, I wanted to punch that guy's face in."

"You did a good job of it," Pops answered. "You gave them something they'll talk about for months. But man, if I were you, I'd watch my back in the locker room. The other guys aren't going to forget you cost them their ticket to the state championship."

"I know," Tommy answered. "I can't believe it myself. I can't believe any of this."

"Relax," Pops said. "You didn't really care about wrestling, anyway. Football's where the glory is."

"No," Nicki heard Tommy answer. "I can't do this. I can't believe you gave this stuff to me and I can't take it anymore. It's freaking me out! I don't even know who I am anymore, but I know I don't take drugs!"

A note of hysteria had crept into Tommy's voice, and Nicki shivered in fright. What if he and Pops began to fight? What could four seventh-grade girls do to stop it?

"Calm down," Pops answered smoothly. "And don't be mad at me. You need me, so get over it. Don't worry, you're taking the safe stuff. Do you think I'd give you anything bad?"

"The safe stuff?"

"Sure. There are some guys who inject themselves with all kinds of testosterone without knowing what they're doing, and that is dangerous." Pops lowered his voice, and Nicki had to strain to hear him. "But I've been doing it for years and I'm fine. This baby stuff you've been taking is okay. Trust me."

Nicki felt a tug at her sleeve. "He's lying," Meredith said, mouthing the words. "There are no safe kinds."

Tommy remained silent for a minute, then Nicki heard concern in his voice. "Pops, you're gonna kill yourself with that stuff."

Pops laughed. "At least I'll look good in my coffin."

Tommy didn't answer, and Nicki could almost picture him sputtering in confusion.

"I can't do it," Tommy said finally. "It doesn't seem fair to the other guys who work so hard."

"You work hard, too," Pops answered. "I write out your weightlifting program myself, so there's no way you can tell me you haven't earned every inch of those new biceps. And isn't it worth it? Or don't the girls like the new you?"

In the moonlight, Nicki saw Meredith shake her head in disgust. Laura stood with her back against the wall of the shed, obviously terrified, but Christine was facing the building with her arms folded and her lips pressed together.

Uh-oh. If Tommy or Pops says one more stupid thing, Christine will run in there and give them a piece of her mind . . .

Christine's green eyes were glittering in anger and Nicki knew either Tommy or Pops, whichever one Chris lit into,

would be in trouble. The Kelshaw kids sometimes had fero-
cious fights at home, but they always stood up for each other.

A rhythmic creaking noise broke the silence. Nicki closed
her eyes and imagined Pops leaning on a table that squeaked
as he idly pumped a dumbbell.

"Now," Pops said, "about the money you owe me. I can't give
you anymore stuff until you pay me for the package I gave you
yesterday. That'll last you for a few weeks, but if you don't pay me
the fifty dollars, you're going to deflate like a popped balloon."

"Don't worry," Tommy answered, his voice flat. "I have the
money."

Nicki groaned. Christine heard, too, and Tommy's comment
was enough to turn her into a raving redhead. She lunged past
Nicki and leapt into the open doorway before Nicki could put
out a hand to stop her. Nicki did stop the other girls, though.

The tornado of Christine's fury centered on Tommy first.

"Tommy Kelshaw!" she ranted. "You stole that money from Dad
and let Torrie and me take the blame! How could you do that?"

"Where'd she come from?" Pops asked, his voice calm. "Can't
you keep your little sister out of your business?"

"And you!" Christine lit into Pops. "You're nothing but
a creep."

"Go away, little girl," Pops said in a harsher tone. The creaking stopped.

"Don't you mess with her," Tommy warned.

"Keep your hands off me!" Christine yelled.

"You're trespassing," Pops said. "I can do anything to you as long as you're on my property."

"Oh yeah?" Christine managed a laugh. "What are you going to do, call the police? I could tell them a thing or two about what's been going on at the high school. About vitamins that aren't vitamins. About someone selling drugs to the athletes."

"That's enough, Christine," Tommy said. "I don't know how you got here, but you can turn around and go home. I know what I'm doing. Everything's fine."

"No, it's not!" Christine anger shifted into a heartbroken sob. "You haven't been yourself, Tommy. You've been mean and cruel—"

Pops broke in, teasing in a high voice: "Oh, Tommy, have you been a meanie?"

Christine's fury returned. "Tommy, I don't know who you think you are, but you're not Arnold Schwarzenegger! You're Tommy Kelshaw, and lately you've been hurting everyone around you."

"Come on, man." Pops's voice was suddenly impatient. "Get rid of the kid."

Christine's voice softened. "You're my big brother, Tommy, and I love you, not the pumped-up superjock you think you are."

"This is getting deep," Pops said, mocking Christine. "Maybe you're forgetting why you took up weight training in the first-place. Remember your spot on the varsity football team?

Remember that cute little cheerleader who won't be happy unless you play varsity?"

Listening outside, Nicki's heart knocked against her rib cage. If Christine lost this argument, should she, Meredith, and Laura go in? Should they run for the limo and have Mr. Peterson call the police? Suddenly, their original plan seemed silly. What had they hoped to do? They had wanted to talk to Tommy, but now there was nothing they could say that Christine hadn't already said. From this point on, Nicki realized, it was all up to Christine. Either she or Pops would win.

"Tommy," Christine said, lowering her voice, "you put your hand through the kitchen wall the other night. Do you remember? But we covered for you because we knew there had to be a good reason. And then, in the garage, you scared me. You could have really hurt me. Don't you realize that?"

Tommy mumbled something Nicki couldn't hear.

"And tonight," Christine went on, "you broke Richie Stevens's nose and your entire team lost the match because you blew it. When you're taking those pills, you can't control your temper. You're out of control and I don't even know you."

"No problem, man," Pops interrupted. "We can fix that. The dose was probably too high, so we'll cut back enough to cool the problem."

Nicki couldn't stand being in the dark any longer, so she slipped to the front of the shed and crouched near the ground. Peeking around the corner, she could see Pops standing in front of a bench rigged with leg weights; apparently, that was the creaking sound she'd heard. Behind Pops was a table on which were bottles of all sorts, some empty and some full. A clipboard hung behind him on the wall.

Tommy, still wearing his blue wrestling uniform, was sitting on the edge of a stool in the corner. He seemed exhausted. Pops had Christine by the arm, and from the redness of his fingers, Nicki knew his grip was tight.

But Christine hadn't finished. "Tommy, you told me once that you wouldn't take drugs because you were a Christian and you wanted to honor God with your body. Do you think God likes it when you use steroids?"

"Oh brother." Pops sighed. "Now we're bringing God into this? Listen, Charlene, your brother knows what's important. Varsity cheerleaders are important. Looking good is important. Playing on the best team is important. Winning—now that's important. You just go on home and let us work this out."

Pops gave Christine a rough push toward the door, but Tommy reached out and steadied her. "Her name is Christine," he said, his face stony as he stood, "and I'm taking her home now."

Christine began to sputter, but Tommy told her to hush as he steered her toward the door.

"Just one more thing," he said as he turned back to Pops. "We're going to tell my parents what's been going on in the athletics department. About how Coach Doster encourages you to give us steroids, and how you peddle them as vitamins until you know a guy's hooked. And about the unfairness of wrestling matches where most of the guys are strong only because of drugs."

"You'll be sorry," Pops said, eying Tommy. "You won't be able to prove anything. Plus, those muscles you're so proud of will be gone even faster than they pumped up. You'll be worse off than when you started 'cause Coach won't even let you play junior varsity if you rat on him. You're wimping out, man, and soon you're gonna look like a wimp, too. You won't be able to hold your head up."

"That's okay." Tommy looked at Christine. "The Kelshaws have more guts than all your poster hunks put together."

Twenty

The next morning when Christine met Meredith, Nicki, and Laura at their usual corner, she was smiling.

"What happened?" Nicki asked, leading the way to school. "We need to hear the end of the story."

Christine shifted her book bag on her shoulder. "After Mr. Peterson dropped us off at home, Tommy had a long talk with Mom and Dad. He told them everything, and he really thought he was taking vitamins until Pops tried to charge him fifty dollars for another bottle. Then Tommy knew something was going on, but he wasn't sure he wanted to quit. Being on the varsity team meant that much to him."

She looked down for a moment, then smiled. "But being alive means a lot to Tommy, too. He had heard about the damage steroids can do. Plus, he'd already seen that he couldn't control his temper when he was taking those things. The way he punched that guy at the match last night was bad enough, but it could have been much worse. Tommy said he realized all he had been doing was trying to please himself, his coach, and his girlfriend. He had forgotten about pleasing God."

She paused. "Remember that tape measure we found in his room? Tommy gave it back to Mom and said he'd been using it to measure his muscles. He said he realized it was wrong because things got to the point that all he cared about was his body.

"So he told Mom and Dad about how Coach set him up to train with Pops. Dad's meeting with the principal of the school this morning, and then he's going to the police. He's not sure what they can do, but at least they ought to know what's going on."

"What about the missing money?" Laura asked.

"Tommy still had it," Christine explained. "So he gave it back to Dad and apologized. Then Dad apologized to me and Torrie this morning because he had accused us of taking it."

Meredith lifted a brow. "So that's it? It's all over?"

"Not quite." Christine shifted her book bag again. "Tommy might have problems coming off the steroids, so he's going to a counselor my dad knows. Plus, Dad grounded him for two weeks for taking the money. And Tommy's pretty sure Amy's going to dump him because he's not going to play football next year."

"If she does dump him," Laura said, "you tell him he can cry on my shoulder. I think he's a living doll, with or without big muscles."

"I don't think he's sunk that low yet," Christine said, patting Laura's shoulder. "I mean, as low as the seventh grade. When he's twenty-three and you're twenty, though, you two might be perfect for each other."

Laura dimpled. "That's true, isn't it?"

Nicki nodded, mentally going over all the clues. "Well, that's another mystery solved, then. Maybe we can enjoy a few weeks with no problems."

"I don't think so." Laura stopped in midstride so suddenly that Meredith nearly ran into her. "I forgot to tell you. I got an instant message from Kim when I was checking my e-mail last night."

"What did she want?" Meredith asked.

Laura shook her head. "You won't believe it. She wanted me to bring her a bottle of hair color. Kim wants to be a blonde."

Nicki groaned.

—

They weren't sure what Kim would look like when they met her at the lockers, but she looked like ordinary Kim. Her hair was short, but smooth and shiny, and she had combed it into a fashionable hairstyle. She was smiling, and as the girls told her of the previous night's adventure, she shook her head.

"I wish I could have been with you," she said, sighing. "But I am glad I was not."

"What did you do, Kim?" Laura asked. "And why did you want a bottle of hair color?" She crinkled her nose. "Do you really want to be a blonde?"

Kim laughed and closed her locker. "Last night I was unhappy and embarrassed," she said. "I went home and sat in my room crying. Nothing I tried to do to make myself the American girl seemed to work. Instead, as you said, I only looked mixed up. My parents, who are still very Korean, did not know how to help me."

She leaned against the lockers and hugged her books to her

chest. "I thought maybe it was my black hair that caused the problems, so that's when I sent you the message, Laura. But when you didn't respond right away, I had time to think."

She smiled a little smile that brought color to her cheeks. "I thought about how unhappy I was while trying to be like everyone else. I thought nobody except my parents would like me in America."

"How can you say that?" Christine interrupted. "We all like you."

"Very much," Meredith added.

Kim smiled. "You are nice girls," she said. "You made me your friend because you felt sorry for me."

Nicki couldn't argue with that. She still remembered the day months ago when she and her friends had rescued Kim from a verbal attack by Corrin Burns. They had been friends ever since.

"Anyway," Kim went on, "I thought no one could like me, but then I remembered what you told me about Jesus Christ. How He loved everyone, even though they were wicked and foolish. And since I felt very foolish and wicked, I asked Him if He could love me."

She smiled and Nicki saw a new confidence and joy in her eyes. "And I knew then that Jesus does love me and would rule in my heart. And since He loves me, I am no longer foolish or stupid. I may be Korean and different, but that doesn't matter so much now."

Christine leaned forward and gave Kim a hug. "That's great, Kimmie. I'm happy for you."

"Does this mean you don't want to be a blonde anymore?" Laura asked.

"It means," Kim said, "that I am no longer trying to change myself to please people. There are too many people and you cannot please all of them. From now on, I want to learn how to please Jesus."

Nicki thought of Tommy, who last night had come to basically the same decision.

"You're right, Kim," she said. "That is the most important thing."

Meredith nodded. "You have just made the most momentous decision of your life."

"The most what?" Christine asked, crinkling her freckled nose.

"Chris"—Meredith sighed and tossed Christine the worn copy of *More Ways to Increase Your Word Power*—"you need this more than I do."

Be on the lookout for the next exciting adventure of Nicki, Meredith, Christine, Laura, and Kim . . .

The Case of the Teenage Terminator

Pine Grove's track star Jeremy Newkirk has a fear tht is keeping him from competing in the county's annual cross-country race. Without him, Pine Grove Middle School will never win.

What can Nicki and her friends do to help? How can they stop Jeremy's worst nightmare from coming true?

About the Author

Angela Hunt lives in Florida with her husband Gary, their two children, and two big dogs that weigh more than she does! Her favorite hobby is reading and she loves to write stories. You can read more about her and her books at www.angelahuntbooks.com.